P9-DEL-894

HOW I GOT MY SHRUNKEN HEAD

GOOSEBUMPS®
Also available as ebooks

NIGHT OF THE LIVING DUMMY
DEEP TROUBLE
MONSTER BLOOD
THE HAUNTED MASK
ONE DAY AT HORRORLAND
THE CURSE OF THE MUMMY'S TOMB
BE CAREFUL WHAT YOU WISH FOR
SAY CHEESE AND DIE!
THE HORROR AT CAMP JELLYJAM
HOW I GOT MY SHRUNKEN HEAD
THE WEREWOLF OF FEVER SWAMP
A NIGHT IN TERROR TOWER
WELCOME TO DEAD HOUSE
WELCOME TO CAMP NIGHTMARE
GHOST BEACH
THE SCARECROW WALKS AT MIDNIGHT
YOU CAN'T SCARE ME!
RETURN OF THE MUMMY
REVENGE OF THE LAWN GNOMES
PHANTOM OF THE AUDITORIUM
VAMPIRE BREATH
STAY OUT OF THE BASEMENT
A SHOCKER ON SHOCK STREET
LET'S GET INVISIBLE!
NIGHT OF THE LIVING DUMMY 2
NIGHT OF THE LIVING DUMMY 3
THE ABOMINABLE SNOWMAN OF PASADENA
THE BLOB THAT ATE EVERYONE
THE GHOST NEXT DOOR
THE HAUNTED CAR
ATTACK OF THE GRAVEYARD GHOULS
PLEASE DON'T FEED THE VAMPIRE

ALSO AVAILABLE:
IT CAME FROM OHIO!: MY LIFE AS A WRITER by R.L. Stine

Goosebumps®

HOW I GOT MY SHRUNKEN HEAD

R.L. STINE

SCHOLASTIC INC.
NEW YORK TORONTO LONDON AUCKLAND
SYDNEY MEXICO CITY NEW DELHI HONG KONG

If you purchased this book without a cover, you should be aware that this book is stolen property. It was reported as "unsold and destroyed" to the publisher, and neither the author nor the publisher has received any payment for this "stripped book."

No part of this publication may be reproduced, stored in a retrieval system, or transmitted in any form or by any means, electronic, mechanical, photocopying, recording, or otherwise, without written permission of the publisher. For information regarding permission, write to Scholastic Inc., Attention: Permissions Department, 557 Broadway, New York, NY 10012.

ISBN 978-0-545-03518-7

Goosebumps book series created by Parachute Press, Inc.
Copyright © 1996 by Scholastic Inc.

All rights reserved. Published by Scholastic Inc., *Publishers since 1920*. SCHOLASTIC, GOOSEBUMPS, GOOSEBUMPS HORRORLAND, and associated logos are trademarks and/or registered trademarks of Scholastic Inc.

17 16 15   17 18/0

Printed in the U.S.A.   40
First printing, May 2009

"Behind the Screams" bonus material by Matthew D. Payne

Have you ever played *Jungle King*? It's a computer game, and it's really cool. Unless you sink into a quicksand pit or get squeezed to death by the Living Vines.

You've got to be fast to swing from vine to vine without letting them curl around your body. And to grab the shrunken heads that are hidden under trees and bushes.

If you collect ten shrunken heads, you get an extra life. You need a *lot* of extra lives in this game. It's not for beginners.

My friends Eric and Joel play *Jungle King* with me. They are twelve, like me. My sister, Jessica, is eight. She hangs around, but we don't let her play. That's because she always dives into the quicksand pits. She likes the *thwuck thwuck thwuck* sound it makes when your body is being sucked under.

Jessica just doesn't get it.

"Mark, why can't we play a different game?" Joel asked me.

I knew why he wanted to quit. He had just been trampled by a red rhino, the meanest kind.

Joel, Eric, and I were up in my room during our winter break from school, huddled around my computer. Jessica was on the window seat, reading a book. Sunlight poured over her, making her red hair sparkle.

"Kah-lee-ah!" I shouted as I picked up my eighth shrunken head. *Kah-lee-ah* is my jungle cry. It's a word that popped into my head one day. I guess I made it up.

My face was two inches from the monitor screen. I ducked as spears came flying at me from behind a leafy fern.

"Kah-lee-ah!" I let out my battle cry as I picked up another shrunken head.

"Come on, Mark," Eric pleaded. "Don't you have any other games?"

"Yeah. Don't you have any sports games?" Joel demanded. "How about *March Madness Basketball*? That's a cool game!"

"How about *Mutant Football*?" Eric asked.

"I like *this* game," I replied, keeping my eyes on the screen.

Why do I like *Jungle King* so much? I think it's because I love swinging from vine to vine across the sky.

You see, I'm a little chubby. Actually, I'm short and chubby. I'm built sort of like the red rhinos.

And so I guess I like being able to swing so lightly, to fly above the ground like a bird.

Also, it's an *awesome* game.

Joel and Eric don't like it because I always win. In our first game this afternoon, an alligator chewed Joel in half. I think that put him in a bad mood.

"Do you know what game my dad bought me?" Joel asked. *"Battle Solitaire."*

I leaned closer to the screen. I had to get past the biggest quicksand pit. One slip, and I'd be sucked into the sandy slime.

"What kind of game is that?" Eric asked Joel.

"It's a card game," Joel told him. "You know. Solitaire. Only the cards fight each other."

"Cool," Eric replied.

"Hey, guys — I'm in a tough spot here," I said. "Give me a break, okay? I've got to concentrate. I'm right over the quicksand pit."

"But we don't want to play anymore," Eric complained.

I grabbed a vine. Swung hard. Then reached for the next one.

And someone bumped my shoulder. "Owww!"

I saw a flash of red hair and knew it was Jessica. She bumped me again and giggled.

I watched myself tumbling down on the screen. Sucked into the bottomless slime pit.

Thwuck thwuck thwuck. I died.

3

I spun around angrily. "Jessica!"

"My turn!" She grinned at me, her wide, toothy grin.

"Now we have to start all over again!" I announced.

"No way," Eric protested. "I'm going home."

"Me, too," Joel said, pulling his baseball cap lower on his forehead.

"One more game!" I pleaded.

"Come on, Mark. Let's go outside," Joel said, pointing to the bright sunshine pouring through the bedroom window.

"Yeah. It's a great day out. Let's throw a Frisbee or something," Eric suggested. "Or get our skateboards."

"One more game. Then we'll go outside," I insisted.

I watched them head out the door.

I really didn't want to leave the jungle. I don't know why I like jungles so much. But I've been really into jungles since I was a teeny kid.

I like to watch all the old jungle movies on TV. And when we were little, I used to pretend I was Tarzan, King of the Jungle. Jessica always wanted to play, too. So I let her be Cheetah, my talking chimpanzee.

She was very good at it.

But after she was six or seven, Jessica refused to be a chimp anymore. She became a full-time pest instead.

"I'll play *Jungle King* with you, Mark," she offered, after my two friends left.

"No way," I replied, shaking my head. "You just want to take a dive into the quicksand pit."

"No. I'll play it right," she promised. "I'll try to win this time. Really."

I was about to let her play when the doorbell rang downstairs.

"Is Mom home?" I asked, listening for her footsteps.

"I think she's in the backyard," Jessica replied.

So I hurried downstairs to answer the front door. *Maybe Eric and Joel changed their minds*, I thought. *Maybe they've come back for another round of* Jungle King.

I pulled open the front door.

And stared at the grossest thing I ever saw in my life.

I stared at a head.

A human head, wrinkled and leathery. About the size of a tennis ball.

The pale, dry lips were pulled back in a sneer. The neck was stitched closed with heavy black string. The eyes — solid black eyes — stared up at me.

A shrunken head. A real shrunken head.

I was so shocked, so totally *amazed* to find it at my front door, that it took me a long time to see the woman who was holding it.

She was a tall woman, about my mom's age, maybe a little older. She had short black hair with streaks of gray in it. She wore a long raincoat buttoned to the top even though it was a warm, sunny day.

She smiled at me. I couldn't see her eyes. They were hidden behind large black-framed sunglasses.

She held the shrunken head by the hair — thick black hair. Her other hand held a small canvas suitcase.

"Are you Mark?" she asked. She had a soft, smooth voice, like someone in a TV commercial.

"Uh . . . yeah," I replied, staring at the shrunken head. They never looked so *ugly* in photos I'd seen. So wrinkled and dry.

"I hope I didn't startle you with this thing," the woman said, smiling. "I was so eager to give it to you, I took it out of my bag."

"Uh . . . *give* it to me?" I asked, not taking my eyes off it. The head stared back at me with those glassy black eyes. They looked more like teddy-bear eyes than human eyes.

"Your aunt Benna sent it for you," the woman said. "As a present."

She held out the head to me. But I didn't take it. I had spent all day collecting shrunken heads in the game. But I wasn't sure I wanted to touch this one.

"Mark — who's here?" My mom stepped up behind me. "Oh. Hello."

"Hello," the woman replied pleasantly. "Did Benna write and tell you I was coming? I'm Carolyn Hawlings. I work with her. On the island."

"Oh, my goodness!" Mom exclaimed. "Benna's letter must have gotten lost. Come in. Come in."

She pulled me back so that Carolyn could enter the house.

"Look what she brought for me, Mom," I said. I pointed to the small green head dangling by the hair from Carolyn's hand.

"Yuck!" Mom cried, raising a hand to her cheek. "That isn't real — *is* it?"

"Of course it's real!" I cried. "Aunt Benna wouldn't send a *fake* — would she?"

Carolyn stepped into the living room and set down her small suitcase. I took a deep breath. Worked up my courage. And reached for the shrunken head.

But before I could take it, Jessica swooped in — and grabbed it out of Carolyn's hand.

"Hey!" I shouted, reaching for her.

She darted away, giggling, her red hair flying behind her. Holding the head in both hands.

But then she stopped.

Her smile faded. And she stared down at the head in horror.

"It bit me!" Jessica cried. "It *bit* me!"

I gasped. Mom squeezed my shoulder.

Jessica started to giggle.

One of her dumb jokes.

She tossed the head from hand to hand. And grinned at me. "You're dumb, Mark. You'll believe anything."

"Just give me back my head!" I cried angrily. I dove across the living room and grabbed for it.

She started to pull it away — but I held on tightly.

"Hey — you scratched it!" I shrieked.

She did. I held the head up close to my face to examine it. Jessica had scratched a long white line on the right earlobe.

"Jessica — please," Mom begged, crossing her arms and lowering her voice. That's what Mom does when she's about to get steamed. "Shape up. We have a guest."

Jessica crossed her arms and pouted back at Mom.

Mom turned to Carolyn. "How is my sister Benna doing?"

Carolyn pulled off her sunglasses and tucked them into a raincoat pocket. She had silvery gray eyes. She looked older without the dark glasses on. I could see hundreds of tiny wrinkles at the corners of her eyes.

"Benna is fine," she replied. "Working hard. Too hard. Sometimes she disappears into the jungle for days."

Carolyn sighed and started to unbutton her raincoat. "I'm sure you know Benna's work is her life," she continued. "She spends every minute exploring the jungles of Baladora. She wanted to come visit. But she couldn't leave the island. So she sent me instead."

"Well, it's very nice to meet you, Carolyn," Mom said warmly. "I'm sorry we didn't know you were coming. But any friend of Benna's is more than welcome."

She took Carolyn's raincoat. Carolyn wore khaki pants and a short-sleeved khaki shirt. It looked like a real jungle-exploring suit.

"Come sit down," Mom told her. "What can I offer you?"

"A cup of coffee would be nice," Carolyn replied. She started to follow Mom to the kitchen. But she stopped and smiled at me. "Do you like your present?"

I gazed down at the wrinkled, leathery head in my hands. "It's beautiful!" I declared.

That night before going to bed, I placed the head on my dresser. I brushed its thick black hair straight back. The forehead was dark green and wrinkled like a prune. The glassy black eyes stared straight ahead.

Carolyn told me that the head was over one hundred years old. I leaned against the dresser and stared at it. It was so hard to believe that it had once belonged to a real person.

Yuck.

How had the guy lost his head? I wondered.

And who decided to shrink it? And who kept it after it was shrunk?

I wished Aunt Benna were here. She would explain everything to me.

Carolyn was sleeping in the guest room down the hall. We had sat in the living room, talking about Aunt Benna all night. Carolyn described the work Aunt Benna was doing on the jungle island. And the amazing things she was finding there on Baladora.

My aunt Benna is a pretty famous scientist. She has been on Baladora for nearly ten years. She studies the animals in the jungle. And the plant life, too.

I loved listening to Carolyn's stories. It was

11

as if my *Jungle King* computer game had come to life.

Jessica kept wanting to play with my shrunken head. But I wouldn't let her. She had already put a scratch on its ear.

"It's not a toy. It's a human head," I told my sister.

"I'll trade you two of my Koosh balls for it," Jessica offered.

Was she *crazy*?

Why would I trade a valuable treasure like this for two Koosh balls?

Sometimes I worried about Jessica.

At ten o'clock, Mom sent me up to my room. "Carolyn and I have some things to talk about," she announced. I said good night and made my way upstairs.

I changed into my pajamas and looked at the head on my dresser. Its dark eyes appeared to flash for a second when I turned out the lights.

I climbed into bed and pulled up the covers. Silvery moonlight washed into the room from the bedroom window. In the bright moonlight, I could see the head clearly, staring at me from the dresser top, bathed in shadows.

What a horrible sneer on its face, I thought with a shiver. *Why is it locked in such a frightening expression?*

I answered my own question: *You wouldn't smile either, Mark, if someone shrunk your head!*

I fell asleep staring at the ugly little head.

I slept heavily, without any dreams.

I don't know how long I slept. But sometime in the middle of the night, I was awakened by a terrifying whisper.

"Mark . . . Mark . . ."

"Mark . . . Mark . . ."

The eerie whisper grew louder.

I sat straight up, and my eyes shot open. And in the heavy darkness, I saw Jessica, standing beside the bed.

"Mark . . . Mark . . . ," she whispered, tugging my pajama sleeve.

I swallowed hard. My heart pounded. "Huh? You? What's your problem?"

"I — I had a bad dream," she stammered. "And I fell out of bed."

Jessica falls out of bed at least once a week. Mom says she's going to build a tall fence around Jessica's bed to keep her in. Or else buy her a king-size bed.

But I think Jessica would just roll around even harder in a big bed and still fall out. My sister is a pest even in her sleep!

"I need a drink of water," she whispered, still tugging my sleeve.

14

I groaned and pulled my arm away. "Well, go downstairs and get it. You're not a baby," I growled.

"I'm scared." She grabbed my hand and pulled. "You have to come with me."

"Jessica!" I started to protest. But why bother? Whenever Jessica has a scary dream, I end up taking her downstairs for a glass of water.

I climbed out of bed and led the way to the door. We both stopped in front of the dresser. The shrunken head stared out at us in the darkness.

"I think that head gave me bad dreams," Jessica whispered softly.

"Don't blame the head," I replied, yawning. "You have bad dreams just about every night — remember? It's because you have a sick mind."

"Do not!" she cried angrily. She punched my shoulder. Hard.

"If you hit me, I won't get you a drink," I told her.

She reached out a finger and poked the shrunken head on one of its wrinkled cheeks. "Yuck. It feels like leather. It doesn't feel like skin."

"I guess heads get hard when you shrink them," I said, straightening the thick tuft of black hair.

"Why did Aunt Benna send you a shrunken head and not send me one?" Jessica asked.

I shrugged. "Beats me." We tiptoed out into the hall and turned toward the stairs. "Maybe it's because Aunt Benna doesn't remember you. The

15

last time she visited us, you were just a baby. I was only four."

"Aunt Benna remembers me," Jessica replied. She loves to argue.

"Well, maybe she thinks that girls don't like shrunken heads," I said. We made our way down to the kitchen. The stairs squeaked under our bare feet.

"Girls like shrunken heads," Jessica argued. "I know I do. They're cool."

I filled a glass with water and handed it to her. She made gulping sounds as she drank. "You'll share your head with me — right?" she asked.

"No way," I told her.

How do you share a head?

We made our way back upstairs in the darkness. I took her to her room and tucked her in. Then I crept back to my room and slipped into bed.

I yawned and pulled the covers up to my chin.

I shut my eyes but opened them again quickly. What was that yellow light across the room?

At first, I thought someone had turned the hall light on.

But squinting across the room I saw that it wasn't a light. The head. The shrunken head — it was glowing!

As if bright flames surrounded it. A shimmering yellow glow.

And in the glow, I saw the dark eyes gleam and sparkle.

And then the lips — the thin, dry lips that had been set in a hard scowl — the lips began to twitch. And the mouth pulled up in a horrifying smile.

"Nooooooo!"

I let out a terrified wail.

Glowing brightly, surrounded by eerie yellow light, the head grinned at me, its dark eyes flashing.

My hands thrashed at the covers. I struggled to pull myself out of bed. But my legs were tangled in the blanket, and I fell with a hard *thud* to the floor.

"Nooooooo!" I cried. My body trembled so hard, I could barely scramble to my feet.

Gazing up, I saw the grinning head float over the dresser. Float into the air. Float toward me like a glowing comet.

No!

I covered my face to shield myself.

When I glanced back up, the shrunken head glowed on the dresser top.

Had I imagined it floating up?

I didn't care. I ran out of the bedroom. "The head! The head!" I shrieked. "It's glowing. The head is glowing!"

Jessica jumped out as I ran past her bedroom. "Mark — what's going on?" she called.

I didn't stop to answer. I kept on running down the hall to Mom and Dad's room. "The head!" I wailed. "The head!" I was so terrified, I didn't know *what* I was doing!

The door was closed. But I shoved it open without knocking. Mom was lying on her back on her side of the bed. My dad was away this week on a business trip. But Mom still slept on her side of the bed.

As I burst in, she sat up and uttered a startled cry. "Mark?"

I ran up beside her. "Mom — the shrunken head — it started to glow!" I cried, my voice high and shrill. "It's glowing, and it — it *grinned* at me!"

Mom stood up and wrapped me in a hug. She felt so warm and soft. I was shaking all over. I suddenly felt as if I were a little boy again.

"Mark, you had a nightmare," Mom said softly. She ran her hand over the back of my hair, the way she used to do when I was little.

"But, Mom —"

"That's all it was. A nightmare. Take a deep breath. Look how you're shaking."

I pulled away from her. I knew it wasn't a nightmare. I'd been wide-awake. "Come and see," I insisted. "Hurry."

I pulled her out into the hall. A light clicked on in Carolyn's room, and her door swung open. "What's happening?" she asked sleepily. She was wearing a long black nightshirt.

"Mark says his shrunken head glowed," Mom reported. "I think he had a bad dream."

"No, I didn't!" I shouted angrily. "Come on. I'll show you!"

I started to pull Mom down the hall. But I stopped when I saw the intense expression on Carolyn's face. She had been sleepy a second ago. But now her eyes were wide, and she was staring at me hard. Staring at my face, studying me.

I turned away from her and nearly bumped into Jessica. "Why did you wake me up?" Jessica demanded.

I pushed past her and led everyone down the hall to my room. "The head glowed!" I cried. "And it smiled at me. Look. You'll see!"

I burst into my room and strode up to the dresser.

The head was gone.

I stared in shock at the bare dresser top.

Behind me, someone clicked on the bedroom light. I blinked in the bright light, expecting the shrunken head to appear.

Where was it?

My eyes searched the floor. Had it fallen and rolled away? Had it floated out of the room?

"Mark — is this some kind of joke?" Mom asked. She suddenly sounded very tired.

"No —" I started. "Really, Mom. The head —"

And then I saw the sly grin on Jessica's face. And I saw that my sister had both hands behind her back.

"Jessica — what are you hiding?" I demanded.

Her grin grew wider. She never could keep a straight face. "Nothing," she lied.

"Let me see your hands," I said sharply.

"No way!" she replied. But she burst out laughing and brought her hands in front of her. And of course she had the shrunken head gripped tightly in her right hand.

"Jessica!" I let out an angry cry and snatched it away from her. "It's not a toy," I scolded her angrily. "You keep your paws off it. Hear?"

"Well, it wasn't glowing," she sneered. "And it wasn't smiling, either. You made that all up, Mark."

"Did not!" I cried.

I examined the head. Its dry lips were pulled back in the toothless snarl it always had. The skin was green and leathery, not glowing at all.

"Mark, you had a bad dream," Mom insisted, covering her mouth as she yawned. "Put the head down, and let's all get some sleep."

"Okay, okay," I muttered. I flashed Jessica another angry look. Then I set the shrunken head down on the dresser.

Mom and Jessica walked out of my room. "Mark is such a jerk," I heard Jessica say, just loud enough for me to hear. "I asked him to share the shrunken head, and he said he wouldn't."

"We'll talk about it in the morning," Mom replied, yawning again.

I started to turn off the light. But I stopped when I saw Carolyn, still standing in the hall. Still staring hard at me, a really intense expression on her face.

She narrowed her silvery eyes at me. "Did you really see it glow, Mark?" she asked softly.

22

I glanced at the head. Dark and still. "Yeah. I did," I replied.

Carolyn nodded. She seemed to be thinking hard about something. "Good night," she murmured. Then she turned and padded silently back to the guest room.

The next morning, Mom and Carolyn greeted me with the biggest surprise of my life.

"Your aunt Benna wants you to come visit her in the jungle," Mom announced at breakfast.

I dropped the spoon into my Froot Loops. My mouth fell open to my knees. "Excuse me?"

Mom and Carolyn grinned at me. I guess they enjoyed shocking me. "That's why Carolyn came," Mom explained. "To take you back with her to Baladora."

"Wh-why didn't you *tell* me?" I shrieked.

"We didn't want to tell you until we worked out all the details," Mom replied. "Are you excited? You get to visit a real jungle!"

"Excited isn't the word!" I exclaimed. "I'm . . . I'm . . . I'm . . . *I don't know what I am!*"

They both laughed.

"I get to go, too!" Jessica declared, bouncing into the kitchen.

I let out a groan.

"No, Jessica. You can't go this time," Mom said,

putting a hand on my sister's shoulder. "This is Mark's turn."

"That isn't fair!" Jessica wailed, shoving Mom's hand away.

"Yes, it is," I replied happily. "Kah-lee-ah!" I cheered. Then I leaped to my feet and did a celebration dance around the kitchen table.

"Not fair! Not fair!" Jessica chanted.

"Jessica, remember: you don't *like* jungles," I said.

"Yes, I do!" she insisted.

"Next time will be your turn," Carolyn said, taking a long sip of coffee. "I'm sure your aunt would love to show you the jungle, Jessica."

"Yeah. When you're older," I sneered. "You know, the jungle is too dangerous for a kid."

Of course, when I said that to my sister, I had no idea of just how dangerous the jungle could be. No idea that I was heading toward dangers I couldn't even imagine.

After breakfast, Mom helped me pack my suitcase. I wanted to bring shorts and T-shirts. I knew it was hot in the jungle.

But Carolyn insisted that I pack long-sleeved shirts and jeans, because of the scratchy weeds and vines we'd be walking through. And because of all the jungle insects.

"You have to protect yourself from the sun," Carolyn instructed. "Baladora is close to the equator. The sun is very strong. And the temperature stays in the nineties all day."

Of course I carefully packed the shrunken head. I didn't want Jessica to get her paws on it while I was away.

I know, I know. Sometimes I'm pretty mean to my sister.

As we drove to the airport, I thought about poor Jessica, staying home while I went off to exciting adventures with Aunt Benna.

I decided to bring her back a really cool souvenir from the jungle. Some poison ivy, maybe. Or some kind of poisonous snake. Ha-ha!

At the airport, Mom kept hugging me and telling me to be careful. Then she hugged me some more. It was really pretty embarrassing.

Finally, it came time for Carolyn and me to board the plane. I felt scared and excited and glad and worried — all at once!

"Be sure to send postcards!" Mom called as I followed Carolyn to the gate.

"If I can find a mailbox!" I called back.

I didn't think they *had* mailboxes in the jungle.

The flight was very long. So long, they showed three movies in a row!

Carolyn spent a lot of time reading through her notebooks and papers. But when the flight attendants served dinner, she took a break. And she told me about the work Aunt Benna had been doing in the jungle.

Carolyn said that Aunt Benna had made many exciting discoveries. She had discovered two kinds of plants that no one had ever seen before. One is a kind of crawling vine that she named after herself. *Benna-lepticus.* Or something like that.

Carolyn said that Aunt Benna was exploring parts of the jungle where no one had ever gone. And that she was turning up all kinds of jungle secrets. Secrets that will make Aunt Benna famous when she decides to announce them.

"When was the last time your aunt visited you?" Carolyn asked. She struggled to pull open the plastic wrapping around her utensils.

"A long time ago," I told her. "I can hardly remember what Aunt Benna looks like. I was only four or five."

Carolyn nodded. "Did she give you any special presents?" she asked. She pulled out the plastic knife and started to spread butter on her dinner roll.

I scrunched up my face, thinking hard. "Special presents?"

"Did she bring you anything from the jungle when she visited you?" Carolyn asked. She lowered the dinner roll to the tray and turned to me.

She had her dark glasses on again, so I couldn't see her eyes. But I had the feeling she was staring at me, studying me.

"I don't remember," I replied. "I know she didn't bring me anything as cool as a shrunken head. That head is really awesome!"

Carolyn didn't smile. She turned back to her food tray. I could tell she was thinking hard about something.

I fell asleep after dinner. We flew all night and landed in Southeast Asia.

We arrived just after dawn. The sky outside the airplane window was a deep purple. A beautiful color I'd never seen before. A big red sun rose slowly through the purple.

"We change planes here," Carolyn announced. "A huge jet like this could never land in Baladora. We have to take a tiny plane from here."

The plane was tiny, for sure. It looked like a toy. It was painted a dull red. It had two red propellers on the slender wings. I searched for the rubber bands that made the propellers spin!

Carolyn introduced me to the pilot. He was a young man in a red-and-yellow Hawaiian shirt and khaki shorts. He had slicked-down black hair and a black mustache. His name was Ernesto.

"Can this thing fly?" I asked him.

He grinned at me from beneath the mustache. "I hope so," he replied, chuckling.

He helped us up metal steps into the cabin. Then he hoisted himself into the cockpit. Carolyn and I filled the cabin. There was only room for the two of us back there!

When Ernesto started the engine, it chugged and sputtered like a power mower starting up.

The propellers began to twirl. The engine roared. So loud I couldn't hear what Ernesto was shouting to us.

Finally, I figured out that he was telling us to fasten our seat belts.

I swallowed hard and stared out the tiny window. Ernesto backed the plane out of the hangar. The roar was so loud, I wanted to cover my ears.

This is going to be exciting, I thought. *It's kind of like flying inside a kite!*

A few minutes later, we were in the air, flying low over the blue-green ocean. The bright morning sunlight made the water sparkle.

The plane bumped and jerked. I could feel the wind blowing it, making us bounce.

After a while, Carolyn pointed out the islands down below. They were mostly green, with ribbons of yellow sand around them.

"Those are all jungle islands," Carolyn told me. "See that one?" She pointed to a large egg-shaped island. "Some people found buried pirate's treasure on that island. Gold and jewels worth millions of dollars."

"Cool!" I exclaimed.

Ernesto leaned over the throttle and brought the plane lower. So low I could clearly make out trees and shrubs. The trees all seemed tangled together. I couldn't see any roads or paths.

The ocean water darkened to a deep green. The engine roared as the plane bounced against strong winds.

"That's Baladora up ahead!" Carolyn announced. She pointed out the window as another island came into view. Baladora was larger than the other islands, and very jagged. It curved around like a crescent moon.

"I can't believe that Aunt Benna is down there somewhere!" I exclaimed.

Carolyn smiled beneath her dark glasses. "She's there, okay."

I glanced to the front as Ernesto turned in his seat to face us. I saw instantly that he had a troubled expression on his face.

"We have a little problem," he said, shouting over the roar of the engine.

"Problem?" Carolyn asked.

Ernesto nodded grimly. "Yes. A problem. You see . . . I don't know how to land this thing. You two will have to jump."

Panic made me gasp. "But — but — but —" I sputtered. "We don't have parachutes!"

Ernesto shrugged. "Try to land on something soft," he said.

My mouth dropped open. My breath caught in my chest. Both hands gripped the arms of the seat.

Then I saw the smile on Carolyn's face. She shook her head, her eyes on Ernesto. "Mark is too smart for you," she told him. "He's not going to fall for a dumb joke like that."

Ernesto laughed. He narrowed his dark eyes at me. "You believed me — right?"

"Ha-ha. No way!" I choked out. My knees were still shaking. "I knew you were kidding," I lied. "Kind of."

Carolyn and Ernesto both laughed. "You're mean," she told Ernesto.

Ernesto's eyes flashed. His smile faded. "You've got to get used to thinking fast in the jungle," he warned.

He turned back to the controls. I kept my eyes out the window, watching the island of Baladora sweep beneath us. Broad-winged white birds swooped over the tangled green trees.

A short strip of land had been cleared near the south shore of the island. Beyond it, I could see ocean waves smacking against dark rocks.

The little plane hit hard as we landed — hard enough to make my knees bounce up in the air. We bounced again on the bumpy dirt landing strip. Then we rolled to a stop.

Ernesto cut the engine. He pushed open the cabin door. Then he helped us out of the plane. We had to duck our heads.

Ernesto carried our suitcases out. Carolyn had her small canvas bag. My suitcase was a little larger. He set them down on the landing strip and gave us a short two-fingered salute. Then he climbed back into the little red plane and pulled the door closed behind him.

I shut my eyes as the propellers whirred, showering dust over me. A few seconds later, Ernesto took off. The plane nosed up steeply, just barely making it over the trees at the end of the landing strip.

The plane turned sharply and headed back over the water. Carolyn and I picked up our bags. "Where do we go now?" I asked, squinting in the bright sunlight.

Carolyn pointed. A clearing of tall grass stretched beyond the narrow dirt airstrip. At the edge of the clearing where the trees started, I could see a row of low gray buildings.

"That's our headquarters," Carolyn told me. "We built the airstrip right next to it. The rest of the island is jungle. No roads. No other houses. Just wilderness."

"Do you get cable?" I asked.

She stopped short. Then laughed. I don't think she expected me to make a joke.

We carried our suitcases toward the low gray buildings. The morning sun was still low in the sky. But the air was already hot and wet. Hundreds of tiny white insects — some kind of gnat — hovered over the tall grass, darting one way, then the other.

I heard shrill buzzing. And somewhere in the distance, the high cry of a bird, followed by a long, sad reply.

Carolyn walked quickly, taking long strides through the tall grass, ignoring the darting white gnats. I jogged to keep up with her.

Sweat ran down my forehead. The back of my neck started to itch.

Why was Carolyn in such a hurry?

"We're kind of trapped here, right?" I said, studying the low, twisted trees beyond the small headquarters buildings. "I mean, how do we get off the island when we're finished?"

"We radio for Ernesto," Carolyn replied, not slowing her pace. "It takes him about an hour to get here from the mainland."

That made me feel a little better. I scurried through the tall grass, struggling to keep up with Carolyn.

My suitcase began to feel heavy. I wiped sweat from my eyes with my free hand.

We were nearing the headquarters. I expected Aunt Benna to come running out to greet me. But I couldn't see any sign of anyone.

A radio antenna was perched off to the side. The low buildings were perfectly square. Flat-roofed. They looked like upside-down cartons. Square windows had been cut in each wall.

"What is that stretched over all the windows?" I asked Carolyn.

"Mosquito netting," she replied. She turned back to me. "Have you ever seen a mosquito as big as your head?"

I laughed. "No."

"Well, you will."

I laughed again. She was joking — right?

We stepped up to the first building, the largest in the row. I set down my suitcase, pulled off my baseball cap, and mopped my forehead with my shirtsleeve. Wow. It was hot.

A screen door led into the building. Carolyn held it open for me.

"Aunt Benna!" I cried eagerly. Leaving the suitcase on the ground, I ran inside. "Aunt Benna?"

Sunlight filtered through the netting over the window. It took a few seconds for my eyes to adjust to the darker light.

I saw a table cluttered with test tubes and other equipment. I saw a bookshelf against a wall, filled with notebooks and books.

"Aunt Benna?"

Then I saw her. Wearing a white lab coat. Standing with her back to me, at a sink against the wall.

She turned, wiping her hands on a towel.

No.

Not Aunt Benna.

A man. A white-haired man in a white lab coat.

His hair was thick and brushed straight back. Even in the dim light, I could see the pale blue of his eyes, blue as the sky. Such strange eyes. They looked like blue glass. Like marbles.

He smiled. Not at me.

He was smiling at Carolyn.

He motioned to me by tilting his head. "Does he have it?" he asked Carolyn. He had a scratchy, hoarse voice.

Carolyn nodded. "Yes. He has it." I could see that she was breathing hard. Short, shallow breaths.

Was she excited? Nervous?

A smile crossed the man's face. His blue eyes appeared to twinkle.

"Hi," I said awkwardly. I felt really confused. What did that question mean? What did I have?

"Where is my aunt Benna?" I asked.

Before he could answer, a girl appeared from the back room. She had straight blond hair and the same pale blue eyes. She was dressed in a white T-shirt and white tennis shorts. She appeared to be about my age.

"This is my daughter, Kareen," the man said in his hoarse voice, more like a whisper. "I am Dr. Richard Hawlings." He turned to Kareen. "This is Benna's nephew, Mark."

"Tell me something I don't know," Kareen replied sharply, rolling her eyes. She turned to me. "Hey, Mark."

"Hi," I replied. Still confused.

Kareen flipped her blond hair back over the shoulders of her T-shirt. "What grade are you in?"

"Sixth," I told her.

"Me, too. Except I'm not in school this term. I'm in *this* dump." She frowned at her father.

"Where is my aunt?" I asked Dr. Hawlings. "Is she working or something? I thought she'd be here. You know. When I arrived."

Dr. Hawlings stared at me with those strange blue eyes. It took him a long time to reply. Finally, he said, "Benna isn't here."

"Excuse me?" I wasn't sure I'd heard him correctly. It was hard to understand his raspy voice. "Is she . . . uh . . . working?"

"We don't know," he replied.

Kareen played with a strand of her hair. She twisted it around her finger, staring at me.

Carolyn stepped behind the lab table and leaned her elbows on it. She rested her head in her hands. "Your aunt Benna is missing," she said.

Her words made my head spin.

They were so unexpected. And she said them so flatly. Without any feeling at all.

"She's . . . *missing*?"

"She's been missing for a few weeks," Kareen said, glancing at her father. "The three of us — we've been trying really hard to find her."

"I — I don't understand," I stammered. I shoved my hands into my jeans pockets.

"Your aunt is lost in the jungle," Dr. Hawlings explained.

"But — Carolyn said —" I started.

Dr. Hawlings raised a hand to silence me. "Your aunt is lost in the jungle, Mark."

"But — but why didn't you tell my mom?" I asked, confused.

"We didn't want to worry her," Dr. Hawlings replied. "Benna's your mom's sister, after all. So Carolyn brought you here because *you* can help us find her."

"Huh?" My mouth dropped open in shock. "Me? How can I help?"

Dr. Hawlings stepped across the small room toward me. His eyes locked on mine. "You can help us, Mark," he said in his hoarse whisper. "You can help us find Benna — because you have Jungle Magic."

"I have *what*?"

I stared at Dr. Hawlings. I didn't know what he was talking about.

Was *Jungle Magic* some kind of computer game? Was it like *Jungle King*?

Why did he think I had it?

"You have Jungle Magic," he repeated, staring back at me with those amazing blue eyes. "Let me explain."

"Daddy, give Mark a break," Kareen interrupted. "He's been flying for a hundred hours. He must be wrecked!"

I shrugged. "Yeah. I'm a little tired."

"Come sit down," Carolyn said. She led me over to a tall stool beside the lab table. Then she turned to Kareen. "Do we have any Cokes left?"

Kareen pulled open a small refrigerator against the back wall. "A few," she replied, bending down to get to the bottom shelf. "Ernesto is supposed to bring another carton on his next flight."

Kareen brought me a can of Coke. I popped it open and tilted the can to my mouth. The cold liquid felt so good in my hot, dry throat.

Kareen leaned against the table, close to me. "Have you ever been to a jungle before?"

I swallowed more Coke. "No. Not really. But I've seen a lot of jungle movies."

Kareen laughed. "It's not like in the movies. I mean, there aren't herds of gazelles and elephants gathering at the water hole. At least, not on Baladora."

"What animals are on the island?" I asked.

"Mosquitoes, mostly," Kareen answered.

"There are some beautiful red birds," Carolyn said. "Called scarlet ibises. You won't believe their color. Kind of like flamingos, only much brighter."

Dr. Hawlings had been studying me the whole while. He walked over to the table and dropped down onto a stool across from me.

I held the cold soda can against my hot forehead. Then I lowered it to the table. "Tell me about my aunt Benna," I said to him.

"Not much to tell," Dr. Hawlings replied, frowning. "She was studying a new kind of tree snail. Somewhere on this end of the jungle. But one night she didn't return."

"We're very worried about her," Carolyn said, twisting a strand of hair. She bit her lower lip. "Very worried. We searched and searched. Then we decided you could help us."

"But how can I help?" I demanded. "I told you — I've never been to a jungle."

"But you have Jungle Magic," Carolyn replied. "Benna gave it to you. The last time she visited you. We read about it. It's in Benna's notebooks over there."

Carolyn pointed to a stack of black notebooks on the bookshelf against the wall. I gazed at them, thinking hard. I still didn't understand.

"Aunt Benna gave me some kind of magic?" I asked.

Dr. Hawlings nodded. "Yes, she did. She was afraid the secret might fall into the wrong hands. So she gave it to you."

"Don't you remember?" Carolyn asked.

"I was so little," I told them. "I was only four. I don't remember. I don't think she gave me anything."

"But she *did*," Carolyn insisted. "We know you have Jungle Magic. We know that you —"

"How?" I interrupted. "How do you know I have it?"

"Because you saw the shrunken head glow," Carolyn replied. "The head will only glow for people who have the magic. We read that in Benna's notebooks."

I swallowed hard. My throat suddenly felt dry again. My heart began to race.

"You're telling me I have some special kind of magic powers?" I asked in a tiny voice. "But I

41

don't feel strange or anything. I've never done anything magic!"

"You have the magic," Dr. Hawlings said softly. "The magic is hundreds of years old. It belonged to the Oloyan people. They used to live on this island."

"They were headshrinkers," Carolyn added. "Hundreds of years ago. That head I brought you — it was Oloyan. We have uncovered many others."

"But your aunt uncovered the secret of their ancient magic," Dr. Hawlings said. "And she gave it to you."

"You've *got* to help us find her!" Kareen declared. "You've got to use the magic. We've got to find poor Benna — before it's too late."

"I — I'll try," I told them.

But secretly, I thought, *They've made a big mistake.*

Maybe they mixed me up with someone else.

I don't have any Jungle Magic. None at all.

What am I going to do?

I spent the day exploring the edge of the jungle with Kareen. We uncovered some amazing yellow spiders that were nearly as big as my fist. And Kareen showed me a plant that can snap its leaves closed around an insect and keep it trapped for days until the plant has digested it all.

Pretty cool.

We climbed low, smooth-barked trees. We sat in the tree limbs and talked.

Kareen is okay, I think. She's very serious. She doesn't laugh a whole lot. And she doesn't like the jungle at all.

Kareen's mom died when she was a little kid. She wants to go back to New Jersey and live with her grandmother. But her father won't let her.

As I talked with her, I kept thinking about Jungle Magic. And I kept thinking about how — whatever it was — I didn't have it.

Sure, I've always liked jungle movies. And jungle books and jungle games. I've always thought jungles are really awesome. But that doesn't mean I have any special powers or anything.

And now Aunt Benna was missing. And her friends on Baladora were so desperate to find her, they had brought me here.

But what could I do?

What?

As I lay in bed that night, the questions didn't go away.

I stared up at the low ceiling of the small wooden shack, wide-awake. There were six or seven flat-roofed shacks in a row behind the main building. We each had our own little shack to sleep in.

My little cabin had a narrow bed with a flat, lumpy mattress. A low bedside table where I placed my shrunken head. A small dresser with all the drawers stuck except the bottom one. A narrow closet, just big enough for the clothes I'd brought. And a tiny bathroom in the back.

Through the netting over the open window, I could hear the chirp of insects. And in the distance, I heard a *caww caww cawww*. Some sort of bird cry.

How can I help find Aunt Benna? I wondered as I stared up at the dark ceiling and listened to the strange sounds.

What can I do?

I tried to remember her. I tried to remember her visit to my house when I was four.

I pictured a short, dark-haired woman. Chubby like me. A round pink face. Intense dark eyes.

I remembered that she talked very fast. She had sort of a chirpy voice, and she always seemed excited. Very enthusiastic.

And I remembered . . .

Nothing else.

That's all I could remember about my aunt.

Did she give me Jungle Magic? No. I didn't remember anything about that.

I mean, how do you give someone *magic*?

I kept thinking about it and thinking about it. I struggled to remember more about her visit.

But I couldn't.

I knew that Carolyn and Dr. Hawlings had made a terrible mistake. *I'll tell them in the morning*, I decided. *I'll tell them they got the wrong kid.*

A terrible mistake . . . terrible mistake. The words repeated in my mind.

I sat up. No way I could get to sleep. My brain wouldn't let me. I was wide-awake.

I decided to take a walk around the headquarters building. Maybe explore back where the trees grew thick and the jungle started.

I crept to the screen door and peered out. My little cabin stood at the end of the row. I could see the other cabins from my door. All dark. Kareen, Carolyn, and Dr. Hawlings had gone to sleep.

Cawwww cawwwww. The strange cry repeated in the distance. A soft wind made the tall grass bend and shift. Tree leaves rustled, making a whispering sound.

I was wearing a long, baggy T-shirt pulled down over boxers. *No need to get dressed,* I decided. *No one else is awake. Besides, I'll just take a very short walk.*

I slipped into my sandals. Pushed open the screen door. And stepped outside.

Cawwww cawwwww. The cry sounded a little closer.

The night air felt hot and wet, nearly as hot as during the day. A heavy dew had fallen, and my sandals slid over the damp, tall grass. The wet grass tickled my feet through the sandals.

I made my way past the silent, dark shacks. To my right, the trees bent and swayed. Black shadows against a purple sky. No moon. No stars tonight.

Maybe taking a walk is a bad idea, I told myself. *Maybe it's too dark.*

I need a flashlight, I realized. I remembered Carolyn's warning earlier when she showed me where I would sleep. "Never go out at night without a flashlight. At night," she had warned me, "we are not in charge here. At night, this is the creatures' world."

The back of the headquarters building loomed ahead of me. I decided to turn around.

But before I could turn, I realized I wasn't alone.

In the semidarkness, I saw a glint: a pair of eyes staring back at me.

I gasped. A chill ran down my back.

Staring hard through the purple night, I saw another pair of eyes.

And then another and another.

Dark eyes, staring at me without moving, without blinking.

Dark eyes, on top of each other.

I froze. I couldn't move.

I knew that I was trapped. There were too many of them. Too many.

My legs trembled. Chill after chill rolled down the back of my neck.

And as I stared at the eyes, the dark eyes in pairs, eyes on top of eyes — as I stared at them, they began to glow.

Brighter. Brighter.

And in the golden light, I saw that these were not creature eyes.

These were not animal eyes.

These were human eyes.

I stared at the glowing eyes of a hundred shrunken heads!

A pile of shrunken heads. All heaped together. Heads like tight fists, mouths curled into snarls or open in toothless horror.

Heads on heads. Dark and wrinkled and leathery.

So terrifying in the cold golden glow from their eyes.

I uttered a choked cry — and took off.

My legs felt rubbery and weak. My heart pounded in my chest. I ran around the headquarters building, the yellow glow fading slowly from my eyes. I ran as fast as I could. To the front of the dark building. To the screen door.

Gasping for breath, I pulled open the door. And leaped inside.

I pressed my back against the wall and waited. Waited for the eerie glow to fade completely. Waited for my heart to stop racing, for my breathing to slow.

After a minute or two, I began to feel a little calmer.

Those heads, I wondered. *Why are they piled back there like that?*

I shook my head hard, trying to lose the ugly picture of them. *They were all people once,* I realized. *Hundreds of years ago, they were people.*

And now . . .

I swallowed hard. My throat felt tight and dry.

I started across the room to the refrigerator. *I need something cold to drink,* I told myself. I bumped the edge of the lab table.

My hands shot out, and I knocked something over. I grabbed it before it rolled off the table.

A flashlight.

"Hey!" I cried out happily.

I'm going to listen to Carolyn's advice from now on, I promised myself. *I'm never going out again without a flashlight.*

I pushed the button, and a white beam of light swept over the floor. As I raised the flashlight, the light settled on the bookshelf against the wall.

Aunt Benna's black notebooks flashed into view. A tall stack of them nearly filled the shelf.

I moved quickly to the bookshelf. With my free hand, I pulled down the top notebook. It was heavier than I thought, and I almost dropped it.

Cradling it in my arms, I carried it over to the lab table. I climbed onto the tall stool and opened it up.

Maybe I can find some answers in here, I thought.

Maybe I can find the part where Aunt Benna talks about giving me Jungle Magic. Maybe I can find out why Dr. Hawlings and Carolyn think I have it.

I leaned over the notebook and aimed the light onto the pages. Then I began flipping through, page after page, squinting in the light.

Luckily, my aunt has big, bold handwriting. Very clean and easy to read.

The pages seemed to be organized by year. I kept flipping pages, scanning each page quickly — until I came to the year of her visit.

My eyes rolled down over a long section about lizards. Some kind of tree lizards that Aunt Benna was studying.

Then she described a cave she had found, cut into the rocky shore at the other side of the island. The cave, she wrote, had been lived in by the Oloyans, maybe two hundred years ago.

I skimmed over long lists of things Aunt Benna had found in the cave. Her handwriting got very jagged, very crooked here. I guess she was really excited by her discovery.

I turned several more pages. And started a section marked "Summer."

As I read the words, my mouth dropped open. My eyes nearly bulged out of my head.

The words started to blur. I lowered the flashlight to the page so that I could see better. I blinked several times.

I didn't want to believe what I was reading.

I didn't want to believe what Aunt Benna had written.

But the words were there.

And they were terrifying.

The flashlight shook in my hand. I steadied it between both hands. Then I leaned forward and read Aunt Benna's words, moving my lips silently as I read.

"Dr. Hawlings and his sister, Carolyn, will stop at nothing to destroy the jungle and all the creatures who live here," my aunt wrote in her bold, clear handwriting. "They do not care who they hurt or who they kill. They care only about getting what they want."

I swallowed hard. Steadied the circle of light over the notebook page. And kept reading.

"Finding the secret of Jungle Magic in that cave was my most amazing discovery," Aunt Benna wrote. "But I know the secret is not safe as long as Dr. Hawlings and Carolyn are around. They will use the Jungle Magic to do evil. And so I have given the Jungle Magic and its secret to my nephew, Mark. He lives four thousand miles away in the United States. And so I hope the secret will be safe.

"If the Jungle Magic ever falls into Hawlings's hands," my aunt continued, "the jungle will be destroyed. The island of Baladora will be destroyed. And so will I."

I gasped and turned the page. I struggled to keep the flashlight steady so that I could read more.

"If Hawlings gets the Jungle Magic," Aunt Benna wrote, "he will shrink my head until there is no trace of me. I must keep my nephew four thousand miles away from Hawlings. Because he will shrink Mark's head, too, to get at the magic I have hidden there."

"Ohhhh." A terrified moan escaped my throat.
Shrink my head?
Dr. Hawlings will shrink my head?

I read the last words again: "I must keep my nephew four thousand miles away . . ."

But I'm not four thousand miles away! I told myself.

I'm here. I'm right here!

Carolyn brought me here to steal the magic. To take it from me. She and Dr. Hawlings planned to shrink my head!

I slammed the notebook shut. I took a deep breath and held it. But it didn't help to slow the thudding of my heart.

What have they done to Aunt Benna? I wondered.

Did they try to get the secret from her? Did they do something terrible to her?

Or did she run away from them? Did she escape?

Did they bring me here to track her down so that they could capture her again? Then when I find her, do they plan to shrink both of our heads?

"Nooooo," I murmured, trying to stop my body from trembling.

I thought they were my friends. My friends . . .

But I'm not safe here, I told myself. *I'm in terrible danger.*

I have to get away. Get dressed and get away from these evil people. As fast as I can.

I dropped off the stool, turned, and started toward the door.

Got to get out. Got to get away.

The words repeated in rhythm with my pounding heart.

I reached for the screen door. Started to push it open.

But someone was standing there. Standing there in the deep shadows, blocking my escape.

"Where do you think you're going?" a voice called.

Kareen pulled open the door and stepped into the room. She wore an oversized T-shirt, down past her knees. Her blond hair was wild about her face. "What are you doing in here?" she demanded.

"Let me go!" I cried. I raised the flashlight like a weapon.

She took a step back. "Hey!" She let out a startled cry.

"I have to go," I insisted, pushing past her.

"Mark — what's your problem?" she asked. "Why are you acting so crazy?"

I stopped with the screen door half open, my shoulder against the frame. "I saw Aunt Benna's notebook," I told Kareen, shining the flashlight beam on her face. "I read what Aunt Benna said. About your father. And about Carolyn."

"Oh." Kareen let out a long sigh.

I kept the harsh light on her face. She squinted at me, then covered her eyes with her arm. "Where is my aunt?" I demanded sharply. "Do you know where she is?"

"No," Kareen replied. "Lower the light — okay? You don't have to blind me."

I lowered the light. "Did your father do something terrible to my aunt? Did he hurt Aunt Benna?"

"No!" Kareen screamed. "How can you ask that, Mark? My father isn't evil. He and Benna just don't agree about some things."

"You're sure you don't know where my aunt is? Is she hiding somewhere? Hiding from your father? Is she still on the island?" The questions leaped out of me. I wanted to grab Kareen and force her to tell me the truth.

She tugged at both sides of her blond hair. "We don't know where your aunt is. We really don't," she insisted. "That's why Carolyn brought you here. To help us find her. We're worried about Benna. We really are."

"That's a lie!" I cried angrily. "I read my aunt's notebook. Your father isn't worried about my aunt."

"Well, I am," Kareen insisted. "I like your aunt a lot. She's been really nice to me. I don't care about Daddy and Aunt Carolyn and their arguments with Benna. I'm worried about Benna. I really am."

I raised the flashlight again. I wanted to check

out Kareen's expression. I wanted to see if she was telling the truth.

Her blue eyes flashed in the light. I saw a teardrop running down one cheek. I decided she was being honest with me.

"Well, if you're worried about my aunt, help me get away from here," I said, lowering the light again.

"Okay, I'll help you," she answered quickly, without having to think about it.

I pushed open the screen door and crept outside. Kareen followed. She closed the door silently behind her. "Turn off the light," she whispered. "We don't want Daddy or Carolyn to see."

I clicked off the light and started through the wet grass toward my cabin, walking fast. Kareen hurried to keep at my side.

"I'll get dressed," I whispered. "Then I'm going to try to find Aunt Benna." A shudder swept down my back. "But how? Where should I go?"

"Use the Jungle Magic," Kareen whispered. "It'll tell you where Benna is. It'll tell you where to go."

"But I can't!" I cried shrilly. "Up until today, I didn't even know I *had* any kind of magic. I'm still not sure I believe it."

"Use the magic —" Kareen whispered, narrowing her eyes at me.

"But I don't know how!" I insisted.

"The magic will guide you," she replied. "I'm sure it will. I'm sure it will show you the way."

I wasn't so sure. But I didn't say anything.

My mind was spinning. Aunt Benna's written words kept weaving through my thoughts.

I should be four thousand miles away, I told myself. *I'm only safe if I'm four thousand miles away.*

Now, how will I escape from Carolyn and Dr. Hawlings?

How?

We were striding down the row of cabins. The air still felt hot and wet, heavy. The sky had darkened to black. There were still no stars, no moon.

I'll get dressed, and I'll get away, I told myself.

Get dressed. Get away.

"Hurry, Mark," Kareen whispered at my side. "Hurry. And don't make a sound. Daddy is a very light sleeper."

My cabin came into view at the end of the row.

But before I could reach it, I heard the soft thud of footsteps in the grass. Rapid footsteps.

Kareen gasped and grabbed my arm. "Oh, no! It's *him!*"

I think I jumped a foot in the air.

Should I run? Try to hide?

If this was a game of *Jungle King*, I'd know the right moves. I'd know how to escape from the Evil Scientist. I'd grab a vine and swing myself to safety. And pick up a few extra lives along the way.

But, of course, this was no game.

I pressed my back against the cabin wall and froze there, waiting to be caught.

The rapid footsteps thudded closer.

I held my breath, but my heart still pounded.

I held my breath — and watched a funny-looking animal hop into view.

Not Dr. Hawlings. But a weird-looking rabbit, with huge ears and big paws that thudded the ground as it hopped.

I watched the weird creature dart away, disappearing between two of the low cabins. "Is it a rabbit?"

Kareen raised a finger to her lips, reminding me to be quiet. "It's a new species of giant rabbit your aunt discovered."

"Very educational," I murmured. "But do I need a nature lesson now?"

Kareen pushed me by the shoulders toward my cabin door. "Hurry, Mark. If my dad wakes up . . ." She didn't finish her sentence.

If he wakes up, he'll shrink my head. I finished the sentence for her in my mind.

My legs suddenly felt as if they were about to collapse. But I forced myself into my dark cabin.

My hands were shaking so hard, I could barely get dressed. I pulled on the jeans I'd been wearing that day. And a long-sleeved T-shirt. And changed into my sneakers.

"Hurry!" Kareen whispered from the door. "Hurry up!"

I wished she'd stop saying that. I jumped every time.

"Hurry, Mark!"

I pulled open my suitcase and grabbed the flashlight I'd brought. Then I started to the door.

"Hurry, Mark. Get going!" Kareen whispered.

I stopped halfway across the cabin. Grabbed the shrunken head. Stuffed it into my T-shirt pocket. Then I pushed open the door and stepped back outside.

Where should I go? What should I do? How could I find my aunt?

A million questions rushed through my mind. My throat felt so dry, it ached. I thought about getting one of those cold Cokes in the lab. But I knew I couldn't risk waking Kareen's father.

We started walking across the wet grass. "Don't turn on the flashlight until you're hidden by the trees," Kareen instructed.

"But where do I go? How do I find Aunt Benna?" I whispered, swallowing hard.

"There's only one path," Kareen told me, pointing to the tangled dark trees at the edge of the clearing. "It will lead you part of the way."

"Then what?" I demanded, my voice shaking.

Her eyes locked on mine. "The Jungle Magic will take you the rest of the way."

Yeah. Sure.

And next week, I'll flap my arms and fly to the moon.

I had the sudden urge to turn around. Go back to my little shack. Go to bed and pretend I never read my aunt's notebook.

But then Kareen and I passed the big pile of shrunken heads. The dark eyes all seemed to stare out at me. Such sad, sad eyes.

I don't want my head to end up on that pile, I decided. *No way!*

I started to jog toward the trees.

Kareen hurried to keep up with me. "Good luck, Mark!" she called softly.

"Th-thanks," I stammered. Then I stopped and

turned to her. "What are you going to tell your dad in the morning?"

Kareen shrugged. The wind blew her blond hair around her face. "I won't tell him anything," she said. "I'll tell him I slept all night. That I didn't hear a thing."

"Thanks," I repeated. Then gripping the flashlight tightly, I turned and ran into the trees.

The path was soft and sandy. The sand felt wet through my sneakers. Vines and big, flat leaves reached over the path. They slapped against my jeans legs as I trotted along.

Tall weeds grew over the path. After a minute or so, it became too dark to see. Had I wandered off the path?

I clicked on the flashlight and shone the light along the ground.

The light swept over the tall weeds, strange ferns, tendrils of vines. The black-trunked trees appeared to lean toward me, reaching for me with their smooth limbs.

No path.

Here I am, I thought, squinting into the pale beam of light. *Here I am, all alone in the jungle.*

Now *what do I do?*

"Ow!"

I swatted a mosquito on my neck. Too late. I could feel the throb of its bite.

Rubbing my neck, I took a few steps through the tall weeds. I kept the circle of light in front of my feet.

Aa-OO-tah. Aa-OO-tah.

A shrill cry — very close by — made me stop.

Night in the jungle belongs to the creatures, I remembered with a shiver.

Aa-OO-tah. Aa-OO-tah.

What *was* it?

Not a giant rabbit. It sounded really BIG.

I spun the light in a circle, keeping it low over the grass and vines. The smooth tree trunks shone purple in the pale light.

I didn't see any animals.

I lowered the light.

My whole body was shaking. Despite the damp heat of the night, I couldn't stop shivering.

A wind made the leaves all flap, the trees bend and whisper.

The jungle was *alive*, I realized.

Insects chittered all around. Fat leaves scraped and cracked. I heard the soft crackle of animal footsteps running over the ground.

Aa-OO-tah. Aa-OO-tah.

What *was* that?

Without realizing it, I had pressed myself against a low tree. I took a deep breath and held it, listening hard.

Was the animal moving closer?

Thick clumps of leaves hung down from the low branches, forming a kind of cave. *I'm protected under here*, I thought, gazing all around. I suddenly felt a little safer, hidden under the thick leaves, under the low branches.

Through my leafy roof, I glimpsed a sliver of white moonlight. It made the leaves gleam like silver.

I clicked off the flashlight and lowered myself to a sitting position on the ground. Leaning back against the smooth trunk, I gazed up at the moon, taking slow, steady breaths.

As soon as I felt calmer, I realized how tired I was. The sleepiness swept over me like a heavy blanket. I yawned loudly. My eyelids seemed to weigh a hundred pounds.

I tried to stay alert. But I couldn't fight the drowsiness.

With the chittering of insects for a lullaby, I leaned my head against the tree trunk and drifted into a deep sleep.

I dreamed about shrunken heads.

Dozens of shrunken heads, the leathery skin purple and green, the black eyes glowing like dark coals, the dry black lips pulled back in angry snarls.

The heads floated and danced through my dream. They darted back and forth like tennis balls. They flew into me, bounced against my chest, bounced off my head. But I didn't feel them.

They bounced and floated. And then the dry lips opened, and they all began to sing. *"Hurry, Mark. Hurry."* That was their song.

The words came out hoarse and raspy. The sound of air rattling through dead leaves.

"Hurry, Mark. Hurry." An ugly, frightening chant.

"Hurry, Mark. Hurry."

The black lips twisted into a sneer as they sang. The coal eyes glowed. The heads — dozens of shriveled, wrinkled heads — bobbed and bounced.

I woke up with the whispered words in my ear.

I blinked. Gray morning light shimmered down through the tree leaves. My back ached. My clothes felt damp.

It took me a few seconds to remember where I was.

The frightening dream stayed in my mind. My hand slid up to my T-shirt pocket. I felt the shrunken head tucked tightly inside.

My face itched.

I reached up to scratch my cheek — and pulled something off it. A leaf?

No.

I squinted at the insect in my hand. A large red ant. Nearly the size of a grasshopper.

"Yuck!" I tossed it away.

My skin tingled. My back itched. Something moved up and down my legs.

I jerked myself up straight. Alert. Wide-awake now.

Itching like crazy. My whole body tingling.

I stared down at myself. Stared down at my jeans and T-shirt.

And started to scream.

16

I jumped to my feet. I thrashed my arms in the air. I kicked my legs.

My body was covered with giant red ants.

Hundreds and hundreds of them. Crawling over my arms, my legs, my chest.

Their prickly legs scratched over my throat and the back of my neck. I pulled a fat one off my forehead. Then another off my cheek.

I reached up and felt them crawling in my hair.

"Ohhhh." A low moan escaped my throat as I slapped at my hair. Swept my hands through it. Watched the big red ants fall to the ground.

I felt them crawl over the backs of my hands. Hot and prickly. So big. And so many of them.

I dropped to my knees, slapping at my chest, pulling the insects off my neck. I began rolling frantically in the tall grass, dripping wet from the heavy morning dew.

I rolled and slapped at myself. Rolled over and over, trying to flatten the insects, trying to kick them off me. I grabbed another handful out of my hair and heaved them into a leafy bush.

I struggled back to my feet, twisting and squirming. Pulling at the big red ants.

But there were too many of them. My skin itched and tingled. Their tiny feet prickled my arms, my legs, my chest.

It itched so badly, I felt I couldn't breathe.

I'm suffocating, I realized. *The ants — they're going to* smother *me!*

"Kah-lee-ah!" I screamed, squirming and slapping. "Kah-lee-ah!"

To my surprise, ants started to drop off my body.

"Kah-lee-ah!" I screamed again.

Ants showered down to the ground. They leaped out of my hair, dropped off my forehead, off the front of my shirt.

I stared in amazement as they fell to the ground. Then they scurried away, climbing over each other, stampeding over and under the tall grass.

I rubbed my neck. I scratched my legs. My whole body still tingled. I still itched all over.

But the big ants were gone. They had all jumped off when I shouted my special word.

Special word.

I glanced down over my shirt, trying to rub away the horrible tingling. Inside my pocket, the shrunken head's eyes glowed. A bright, yellow glow.

"Whoa!" I grabbed the head and tugged it from my pocket. I held it up in front of me.

"Kah-lee-ah!" I shouted.

The eyes glowed brighter.

My special word.

Where did the word come from? I didn't know. I thought I made it up.

But I suddenly knew that the word was the secret behind the Jungle Magic.

The word — and the shrunken head.

Somehow the word brought the Jungle Magic to life. When I shouted it out, the ants jumped off me and hurried away.

I gazed at the glowing little head with new excitement. My heart pounded in my chest. I concentrated on the head, thinking hard.

I *did* have Jungle Magic.

Dr. Hawlings and Carolyn were right.

I had Jungle Magic and didn't know it. And the word *Kah-lee-ah* was the key that unlocked it.

It had helped me get rid of the gross red ants. Would it help lead me to Aunt Benna?

"Yes!" I cried out loud. "Yes!"

I knew that it would. I knew I could find her now.

I was no longer afraid of the jungle and its creatures. No longer afraid of anything that might await me in this hot, tangled jungle.

I had Jungle Magic.

I had it — and I knew how to use it.

69

And now I had to find Aunt Benna.

A red morning sun rose over the treetops. The air was already hot and damp. Birds chirped and twittered on the tree limbs above me.

Holding the flashlight in one hand and the shrunken head in the other, I started to run toward the sun.

I'm going east, I told myself. *The sun comes up in the east.*

Was it the right direction to find my aunt?

Yes. I was sure it was right. *The Jungle Magic will lead me,* I decided. *I just need to follow it, and it will take me to Aunt Benna, wherever she is hiding on this island.*

I ran over fat, leafy vines and low shrubs. I ducked under smooth white tree branches. Broad leaves of huge green ferns slapped at me as I ran through them.

The sun beamed down on my face as I made my way through a wide, sandy clearing. Sweat dripped down my forehead.

"Hey!" I cried out as my feet slipped on the soft sand.

My feet slid. I lost my balance. My hands shot out. The flashlight and the shrunken head flew onto the sand.

"Hey!"

I started to sink.

Sand rolled up over my ankles. Up my legs.

I kicked. I waved my arms wildly.

I pulled up my knees. Tried to step out of the deep sand.

But I was sinking, sinking faster now.

Sand up to my waist.

The more I struggled, the faster I sank.

Deeper, deeper. Down into the pit of sand.

I couldn't move my legs. I had sunk too deep in the hot, wet sand.

The sand crept up over my waist.

There's no bottom, I thought. *I'm going to keep sinking. I'm going to sink down, down until it covers my head. Until I disappear forever.*

My friends Eric and Joel once told me that there is no such thing as quicksand. I wished they were here right now. I could show them how wrong they were!

I opened my mouth to shout for help. But I was too panicked to make a sound. Only a tiny squeak came out.

What good is shouting? I asked myself.

There's no one around for miles. No one who will hear me.

The sand felt thick and heavy as I slid down, down deeper into it. I stretched both hands up over my head, my hands grasping, as if trying to grab on to something.

I tried moving my legs. Tried to pump them, like treading water or pedaling a bike.

But the sand was too heavy. I was in too deep.

My chest heaved with terror now. I gasped in breath after breath.

I opened my mouth once again to call for help.

And had an idea.

"Kah-lee-ah!" I screamed, my voice high and frightened.

"Kah-lee-ah! Kah-lee-ah!"

Nothing happened.

"Kah-lee-ah! Kah-lee-ah!"

I screeched the word at the top of my lungs.

But I continued to sink deeper, deeper into the wet, marshy pit of sand.

"Kah-lee-ah!"

No. Nothing.

I waved my arms over my head. And stared up at the pale blue sky. At the trees at the edge of the clearing.

Nothing but trees as far as I could see.

No one around. No one to help me.

"Oh!" I suddenly realized why the magic word wasn't working. I didn't have the shrunken head. The head had flown from my hand when I fell into the sandpit.

Where was it? Where?

Did it sink into the sand?

My eyes frantically searched the yellow-brown surface. The wet sand bubbled all around me, making a *pock-pock-pock* sound. Like a thick soup.

I sank deeper.

And saw the shrunken head.

It lay on the surface. Its black eyes stared up at the sky. Its hair was tangled beneath it, spread over the sand.

With an excited cry, I stretched out both hands and tried to grab it.

No. Too far away. Just out of my reach. Inches out of my reach.

"*Unnnnh.*" I uttered a low grunt as I struggled to grab it. Stretched out my hands. Stretched. Stretched.

I leaned forward into the sand. Leaned and stretched.

And grabbed for it. Grabbed for it, curling my fingers. Groaning and grunting. Reaching. Reaching across the wet sand.

But no.

I couldn't get it. The head lay a foot from my fingertips.

A foot that seemed a mile.

No way. No way.

My fingers grabbed only air. I couldn't reach it.

I knew I was doomed.

My hands dropped heavily onto the wet sand. I let out a defeated sigh.

My hands made a loud slapping sound as they hit the sand.

And the head bounced.

"Huh?" I uttered a startled cry. My heart started to pound.

I slapped the surface of the wet sand again with both palms.

The head bounced. Closer.

Another hard slap. Another bounce.

The head lay only a few inches away now.

I grabbed it, held it tightly — and joyfully shouted out the word. *"Kah-lee-ah! Kah-lee-ah!"*

At first, nothing happened.

My breath caught in my throat. I froze.

"Kah-lee-ah! Kah-lee-ah!"

I expected to fly up. To be lifted out of the sand-pit. To float magically over to hard ground.

"Jungle Magic — please work! Please work!" I cried out loud.

But I didn't move. I sank a little deeper. The sand crept up over my chest.

I stared at the shrunken head in my hand. The black eyes appeared to stare back at me.

"Help me!" I cried. "Why aren't you helping me?"

And then I saw the vines.

Yellow-green vines creeping over the sand-pit. Moving like long snakes. A dozen twisting, crawling vines, slithering toward me from all directions.

My heart pounded as I watched the vines slither closer. Closer. Until I reached out with my free hand and grabbed for the end of one.

But the vine swept past my hand, moving quickly with surprising force. It wrapped itself around my chest — and started to tighten.

"No!" I uttered a cry of protest. Was it going to strangle me?

Another vine dipped into the sand. I felt it curl around my waist.

"No — stop!" I wailed.

The vines tightened around me. And then they began to pull.

The wet sand made a *thwock* sound as I started to move through it.

Holding the shrunken head in the air, I let the vines tug me through the sand. They pulled hard and fast. The sand flew at my sides.

A few seconds later, the vines tugged me, on my knees, onto hard ground. I let out a happy cry. The vines instantly let go. I watched them pull back, curling quickly into the tall weeds.

I hunched there, struggling to catch my breath, watching until the vines slithered out of sight. Then I pulled myself to my feet.

My legs felt shaky and weak. My whole body trembled from my close call.

But I didn't care. I felt like jumping up and clapping and shouting for joy. The Jungle Magic had worked. The Jungle Magic had saved me once again!

The wet sand clung to my jeans, my shirt, my arms — even my hair! I shook myself furiously. I tucked the shrunken head into my shirt pocket. Then I began slapping at my clothes, brushing off chunks of sand.

Now what? I asked myself, glancing quickly around. The sun had risen high in the sky. The trees and ferns and tall grass gleamed, a shimmering blur of green and gold. The air had grown hot. My shirt clung wetly to my back.

Now what?

How do I find Aunt Benna?

I pulled the shrunken head from my pocket and held it in front of me. "Lead the way," I ordered it.

Nothing happened.

I brushed chunks of sand off its leathery skin. I pried sand from between its thin black lips.

I turned toward the sun and took a few steps. Was I still walking east?

To my surprise, the dark eyes on the shrunken head suddenly started to glow.

What did that mean? Did that mean I was getting close to Aunt Benna? Did it mean I was walking in the right direction?

I decided to test it.

I spun around and started walking back toward the sandpit.

The eyes on the head instantly dimmed back to black.

I turned and started walking north.

The eyes remained dark.

I turned back in the direction of the sun.

Yes! The eyes began to glow again. "Kah-lee-ah!" I cried happily. The head was guiding me to my aunt.

Animals howled and insects chittered loudly as I made my way through the trees and tall weeds. It all sounded like music to me now.

"Aunt Benna, here I come!" I cheered.

I found myself walking deeper into the jungle. I had to keep ducking my head to avoid low branches and thick vines that stretched from tree to tree.

I heard weird bird calls overhead. As if the birds were talking to each other. As I ducked under a low limb, the whole tree seemed to shake. And a thousand blackbirds leaped off the branches, cawing angrily, so many of them they darkened the sky as they flapped away.

I suddenly came to a small clearing that forked into two branches, one to the left, one to the right. Which way should I go?

I held the shrunken head in front of me, watching it carefully. I started to the left.

The eyes grew dark. Wrong way.

I turned and started to the right, watching the eyes begin to glow again.

Was Aunt Benna hiding somewhere in these trees? Was I getting close?

The trees ended suddenly again, and I found myself in a grassy clearing. I squinted in the bright sunlight, my eyes sweeping over the shimmering green grass.

A low growl made me spin back toward the trees.

"Oh!" I let out a sharp cry as I saw the tiger. My legs nearly crumpled under me.

The tiger raised its head in another growl. An angry growl. It pulled back its lips, baring enormous teeth. It arched its back, its yellow-brown fur standing straight on end.

Then with a furious hiss it came charging at me.

The tiger's huge paws pounded over the grass. Its yellow eyes burned into mine.

I glimpsed two little cubs behind it, nestled in the shade of a tree.

"I'm not going to hurt your cubs!" I wanted to cry.

But of course there was no time.

The tiger let out a furious roar as it charged.

The roar drowned out my cry as I raised the shrunken head in front of me in a trembling hand. "Kah-lee-ah!"

My voice came out in a whimper.

I nearly dropped the head. My knees collapsed. I sank to the grass.

The tiger closed in for the kill. Its heavy paws thudded the dirt as it leaped toward me.

The ground felt as if it were shaking.

The ground *was* shaking!

To my horror, I heard a deafening *ripping*

sound. Like Velcro being torn apart. Only a thousand times louder.

I let out a cry as the ground trembled. Shook. Split apart.

The grass tore away. The dirt split in two.

The earth opened up.

And I started to fall. Down into an endless hole in the earth.

Down, down.

Screaming all the way.

"Owww!"

I landed hard on my elbows and knees. Pain shot through my body. I actually saw stars! Hundreds of them, all red and yellow.

Trying to blink them away, I raised myself to my knees.

The shrunken head had bounced out of my hand. I spotted it a few feet away in the dirt. I dove for it, grabbed it up in my shaking hand, and held on to it tightly.

I felt dizzy and shaken. I closed my eyes and waited for the dizziness to pass.

When I opened them, I realized I had fallen into a deep pit. Walls of dirt surrounded me. The blue sky was a small square high above my head.

Jungle Magic had saved me once again. The magic had caused the ground to split open so that I could fall to safety. So that I could escape the tiger.

I heard a low growl above me.

With a frightened cry, I gazed up to the top of the pit. And saw two yellow eyes glaring down at me.

The tiger snarled, baring its teeth.

I didn't escape, I realized.

I'm trapped down here. If the tiger leaps down into the pit, it will finish me off in seconds.

I have nowhere to run. No way to escape.

I fell back against the wall of dirt. I stared up at the snarling tiger. It eyed me hungrily, roaring again. Preparing to leap to the attack.

"Kah-lee-ah!" I cried. "Kah-lee-ah!"

The tiger roared in reply.

I pressed my back against the dirt. Tried to stop my whole body from shaking.

Please don't come down here! I begged silently. *Please don't jump down into this pit!*

The yellow eyes glowed in the sunlight. The silvery whiskers twitched as the tiger snarled its toothy warning.

And then I saw a little yellow-and-black cat face appear at the top of the pit. One of the tiger cubs. It peered down at me over the edge of the grass.

The other cub popped up beside it. It leaned over the pit edge. Leaned so far, it nearly fell in!

The tiger moved quickly. It lowered its head — and bumped the cub away from the edge. Then it picked up the other cub in its teeth and carried it away.

I swallowed hard. I didn't move. My back pressed against the cool dirt, I stared up to the top. Watched the square of blue sky. And waited for the tiger to return.

Waited.

And waited. Holding my breath.

Silence now. So silent I could hear the wind rushing through the tall grass.

A chunk of dirt broke off the pit wall and toppled to the bottom, crumbling as it landed. I kept my gaze on the opening, listening hard, watching for the tiger.

After what seemed like hours, I let out a long whoosh of air. I stepped away from the dirt wall and stretched.

The tiger isn't coming back, I decided.

It only wanted to protect its cubs from me. By now, it has taken them away. Far away.

I stretched again. My heart was still thumping hard in my chest. But I was starting to feel a little more normal.

How do I get out of here? I wondered, gazing at the steep dirt walls. *Can I climb out?*

I tucked the shrunken head back into my pocket. Then I dug both hands into the soft, cool dirt and tried to climb.

I pulled myself up about a foot or two. But then the dirt broke off under my sneakers. It crumbled and fell, sending me sliding back to the bottom.

No. No way. I can't climb out, I realized.

I reached for the shrunken head. *I'll have to use Jungle Magic*, I decided.

The magic got me down here. Now I can use it to get me out.

I raised the head in front of me. But before I could call out the word, darkness fell over the pit.

Is the sun setting already? I wondered.

I gazed up to the top.

No. It wasn't evening. The square of sky that I could see was still bright blue.

Someone stood up there, blocking the sunlight.

The tiger?

A human?

I squinted hard, struggling to see.

"Who — who's there?" I called.

22

A face leaned over the edge, peering down at me. Squinting into the bright sunlight, I saw straight blond hair. Pale blue eyes.

"Kareen!" I shouted.

She cupped her hands around her mouth. "Mark — what are you doing down there?"

"What are *you* doing here?" I cried.

Her hair fell over her face. She brushed it back. "I — I followed you. I was so worried about you!"

"Get me out of here!" I shouted up to her. I tried climbing again. But the dirt slid out from under my sneakers.

"How?" she called down.

"I guess you didn't bring a ladder with you?" I shouted.

"Uh — no, Mark," Kareen sniped.

I guess she doesn't have much of a sense of humor.

"Maybe I could drop a rope down or something," she suggested.

"Rope isn't too easy to find in the middle of the jungle," I reminded her.

She shook her head. Her face tightened into a fretful frown.

"How about a vine?" I called up. "See if you can find a long vine. I could climb up a vine."

Her expression brightened. She disappeared. I waited impatiently. And waited. "Please hurry," I murmured out loud, my eyes on the square opening at the top. "Please hurry."

I heard the squawk of birds somewhere up above. Fluttering wings. More squawking and cawing.

Are the birds frightened? I wondered. *If they are,* why? *Has the tiger returned?*

I pressed against the dirt wall, watching the sky.

Finally, Kareen reappeared. "I found a vine. But I don't know if it's long enough."

"Lower it over the side," I instructed her. "Quick. I have to get out of here. I feel like a trapped animal."

"It was hard to pull it out of the ground," she complained. She began lowering the vine. It looked like a long snake twining down the side of the pit.

It stopped a few feet above my head. "I'm going to jump up and grab it," I told Kareen. "Then I'll try to climb while you pull. Wrap the other end around your waist, okay? Just don't let go of it!"

"Just don't pull me down with you!" she called back.

I waited for her to tie the vine around herself. Then I bent my knees and jumped. I missed the end of the vine by a few inches.

This was one of those times I wished I were tall and thin instead of short and chubby.

But I grabbed the vine on my third try. I wrapped both hands around it.

Then I pressed the soles of my sneakers against the dirt wall. And started to pull myself up, like a mountain climber.

The dirt kept crumbling out from under me. And the vine grew more and more slippery as my hands started to sweat. But with Kareen cheering me on, I scrambled to the top.

I lay in the tall grass for a moment, breathing in the sweet fragrance. It felt so wonderful to be out of that deep hole.

"How did you fall down there anyway?" Kareen asked, tossing her end of the vine to the ground.

"It was easy," I replied. I climbed to my feet and tried to brush the dirt off my clothes.

"But didn't you see that big pit there?" she demanded.

"Not exactly," I told her. I wanted to change the subject. "How did you find me? What are you doing here, Kareen?"

Her blue eyes locked on mine. "I told you: I was worried about you. I — I didn't think you should be all alone in the jungle. So I sneaked away. Daddy was working in his lab. I crept away from the headquarters, and I followed you."

I brushed clumps of dirt from my hair. "Well, I'm glad," I confessed. "But aren't you going to be in major trouble with your dad and Carolyn?"

She bit her lower lip. "Probably. But it will be worth the risk — if we find your aunt."

Aunt Benna!

Trying to survive the quicksand and the tiger, I had nearly forgotten about her.

A shadow rolled over us. The air suddenly grew cooler. I glanced up at the sky. The sun was lowering itself behind the trees.

"It's almost night," I said quietly. "I — I hope we can find Aunt Benna before it gets really dark."

I had already spent one night out in the jungle. I didn't want to spend another.

"Do you know which way to go?" Kareen asked. "Are you just wandering around, hoping to get lucky?"

I pulled the head from my shirt pocket. "This little guy is showing me the way."

"Excuse me?" Kareen's face filled with surprise.

"The eyes light up when I go the right direction," I explained. "At least, I *think* that's why they light up."

Kareen gasped. "You mean, you really *do* have Jungle Magic?"

I nodded. "Yeah. I have it. It's so weird. There's a word I've always said. '*Kah-lee-ah.*' Just a crazy word. I thought I made it up when I was a little kid. But it's the word that makes the Jungle Magic work."

"Wow!" Kareen exclaimed. A grin spread across her face. "That's *awesome*, Mark! That means we really will find Benna. That's so great!"

The shadows over the ground grew longer as the sun dipped lower. I shivered as a cold gust of wind blew over us.

My stomach growled. I couldn't remember when my last meal was. I tried not to think about food. I had to keep moving.

"Let's get going," I said softly. I raised the head in front of me. Then I turned slowly — one direction, then the next — until the eyes began to glow. "This way!" I cried, pointing across the clearing to the trees.

We started walking side by side. The tall grass swished, brushing our legs as we stepped through it. Insects chittered in the trees.

Kareen stared in amazement at the glowing eyes on the leathery head. "Do you really think it's guiding us to Benna?"

"We'll soon find out," I said solemnly.

We stepped into the shifting darkness beneath the tangled trees.

As the sunlight faded, the jungle sounds changed. The birds in the trees stopped chirping. The shrill sawing of the insects grew louder. We heard strange animal howls and cries in the distance, the sound bouncing between the smooth trees.

I hoped the howls and cries *stayed* in the distance!

Dark creatures slithered through the tall weeds and low, fat ferns and shrubs. The shrubs appeared to tremble as night creatures scurried through them.

I heard the warning hiss of snakes. The eerie hoot of an owl. The soft flap of bat wings.

I moved closer to Kareen as we walked. The sounds were all so much more realistic than in my *Jungle King* game!

I'll probably never play that game again after this, I thought. *It will seem way too tame.*

We pushed our way through a clump of tall, stiff reeds. The eyes on the shrunken head dimmed to black.

"Wrong way!" I whispered.

Kareen and I turned until the eyes glowed again. Then we moved forward, making our own path. We stepped over thick vines and pushed through tangles of weeds and low shrubs.

"Ow!" Kareen slapped at her forehead. "Stupid mosquito."

The shrill scratching of insects grew louder, drowning out the crunch of our sneakers over the leaves and vines on the jungle floor.

As the darkness deepened, the eyes on the shrunken head appeared to glow brighter. Like twin flashlights, guiding us through the trees.

"I'm getting kind of tired," Kareen complained. She ducked her head to avoid a low branch. "I hope your aunt is nearby. I don't know how much longer I can walk."

"I hope she's nearby, too," I murmured in reply. I'd had a pretty exhausting day myself!

As we walked, I couldn't help thinking about Aunt Benna and her notebook. I didn't want to make Kareen feel bad. But I had to say something.

"My aunt didn't write very nice things about your dad and Carolyn in her notebook," I said, keeping my eyes at my feet. "I was kind of surprised."

Kareen was silent for a long moment. "That's so horrible," she said finally. "They worked together for so long. I knew they had an argument."

"About what?" I asked.

Kareen let out a sigh. "Daddy has some plans to develop the jungle. He thinks there are valuable minerals here. Benna thinks the jungle should be preserved."

She sighed again. "I think that's what they fought about. I'm not sure."

"The notebook made it seem like your dad is evil or something," I muttered, avoiding her eyes.

"Evil? Daddy?" she cried. "No. No way. He's very strong-minded. That's all. He isn't evil. And I know that Daddy still cares about Benna. He still respects her and cares about her. He's really worried about her. He —"

"Whoa." I grabbed Kareen's arm, interrupting her. "Look." I pointed through the trees.

I spotted a clearing up ahead. And against the gray sky, I could see the black outline of a small shack.

Kareen gasped. "That little house. Do you think —?"

We both crept to the edge of the clearing. Something scurried quickly over my sneakers, but I ignored it.

My eyes were on the tiny dark shack.

As we moved closer, I could see that it was built of tree limbs and sticks. Clumps of fat leaves made the roof. It had no window. But there were narrow openings between the branches.

"Hey!" I whispered. I saw a pale light flicker in one of the openings.

A flashlight? A candle?

"Someone is in there," Kareen whispered, narrowing her eyes at the shack.

I heard a cough.

A woman's cough? Aunt Benna's cough? I couldn't tell.

"Do you think it's my aunt?" I whispered, huddling close to Kareen.

"Only one way to find out," she whispered back.

The shrunken head glowed brightly in my hand. The eerie yellow light splashed over the ground as Kareen and I crept closer.

Closer.

"Aunt Benna?" I called in a tiny voice. I cleared my throat. My heart pounded. "Aunt Benna? Is that you?"

I called again and stepped close to the open doorway of the small shack. I heard a thump inside. Saw a flash of light. And heard a startled cry.

A lantern appeared in the doorway. My eyes went to the pale yellow light. And then moved up to see the woman holding the lantern.

She was short — very short. Only about a foot taller than me, and a little chubby. Her straight black hair was tied back. In the glow of lantern light, I saw that she wore khaki slacks and a khaki safari jacket.

"Who's there?" She raised the lantern in front of her.

"Aunt Benna?" I cried, moving closer. "Is that you?"

"Mark? I don't believe it!" she exclaimed. She came running toward me, the lantern swinging at her side. The light bounced over the tall grass, making shadows dance.

She wrapped me in a hug. "Mark — how did you find me? What are you doing here?" She had a high, chirpy voice, and she talked rapidly, without taking a breath.

She pushed me away from her to study my face. "I don't believe I even recognized you. I haven't seen you since you were four!"

"Aunt Benna — what are you doing out here?" I demanded breathlessly. "Everyone is so worried —"

"How did you get to Baladora?" she asked, gripping my shoulder with her free hand, holding the lantern high with the other. "What are you doing in the jungle? How did you get here?" she cried again.

"I — I used the Jungle Magic," I stammered.

Her eyes went wide. With surprise? With fear?

I suddenly realized she wasn't looking at me. "Hello. Who are you?" Aunt Benna asked quietly, stretching the lantern toward the trees.

Kareen stepped out from the edge of the clearing. In all the excitement, I didn't realize that she had lingered behind.

"That's Kareen," I told my aunt. "Do you know Kareen? Dr. Hawlings's daughter?"

Aunt Benna gasped. She squeezed my shoulder. "Why did you bring her here? Don't you realize —?"

"It's okay," Kareen said quickly. "I was worried about you. That's why I followed Mark."

"She helped me," I explained to Aunt Benna. "Kareen helped me get away from them. From Dr. Hawlings and Carolyn. Kareen helped me get through the jungle."

"But — but —" Aunt Benna sputtered. "You told her about the Jungle Magic?"

"I only came to help!" Kareen insisted. "My father is worried about you. He —"

"Your father wants to *kill* me!" Aunt Benna cried angrily. "That's why I had to run away. That's why I had to leave everything behind and hide in the jungle." She glared at Kareen, her eyes squinting, her face pinched and hard in the yellow lantern light.

"Kareen is okay," I assured her. "She only wants to help, Aunt Benna. Really."

My aunt turned to me. "Carolyn and Hawlings brought you here?"

I nodded. "Yes. To find you. Carolyn brought me this." I pulled the shrunken head from my shirt pocket. It had stopped glowing.

"They told me I had Jungle Magic," I continued. "I didn't know what they meant. I thought they were crazy. Then when I went out to look for you in the jungle, I discovered that I *did* have it."

Aunt Benna nodded. "Yes. You have it, Mark. I gave it to you when I visited you. When you were four. I hypnotized you. And I transferred the Jungle Magic from me to you. To keep it safe."

"Yes. I read your notebook," I told her. "I read about why you gave me the magic. But it didn't say what Jungle Magic is. I only know —"

"It's a powerful force," my aunt replied, lowering her voice. "It's a powerful force that will do your will, carry out your wishes."

Her eyes filled with sadness. "But we cannot talk about it now," she said in a whisper. "We are in danger here, Mark. Real danger."

I started to reply. But I heard rustling, cracking sounds from the trees. Footsteps?

All three of us spun around toward the sound.

To my surprise, Kareen started running across the grass. She cupped her hands around her mouth. "Over here, Daddy!" she shouted. "Over here! I found Benna, Daddy! Hurry!"

I gasped in shock.

No time to run.

A beam of light flickered out from the trees. Behind it came Dr. Hawlings, trotting over the tall grass. He carried a flashlight in one hand. The light swept into my eyes, then moved over Aunt Benna.

Was Dr. Hawlings carrying a gun? Some kind of weapon? I couldn't see. And I didn't want to find out.

I grabbed Aunt Benna's arm and tugged. I wanted to run, to escape into the jungle.

But my aunt refused to move. She seemed frozen in surprise. Or fear.

Kareen's father trotted up to us, breathing hard. Even in the dim light, I could see the pleased smile on his face.

"Good work, Kareen." He patted her shoulder. "I knew that if you helped Mark escape, he would lead us right to his aunt."

Still holding on to Aunt Benna's arm, I stared at Kareen angrily. She had tricked me. She had pretended to be my friend. But the whole time, she was working to help her father.

Kareen stared back at me for a moment. Then she lowered her eyes to the ground.

"Why did you trick me?" I demanded. "Why did you do it, Kareen?"

She raised her eyes to me. "Daddy needs the Jungle Magic," she replied softly.

"But you *lied* to me!" I cried.

"I didn't have a choice," Kareen said. "If your father needed your help, what would *you* do?"

"You did the right thing, Kareen," Dr. Hawlings told her.

He raised the light to Aunt Benna's face. He forced her to cover her eyes. "Did you really think you could hide forever, Benna?" he demanded softly.

"I — I'm sorry," I told my aunt. "It's my fault. I —"

"No." Aunt Benna put a hand on my shoulder. "It's not your fault, Mark. It's my fault. You didn't know anything about any of this. And now I'm afraid I've gotten you into a lot of trouble."

Dr. Hawlings snickered. "A lot of trouble. That's the truth." He stepped up to Aunt Benna. "I want the secret of Jungle Magic. Tell me the secret, Benna. Let me know how it works. And I will allow you and your nephew to leave the island in one piece."

In one piece?

I didn't like the sound of that.

As Dr. Hawlings stared at my aunt, I slipped the shrunken head from my pocket. *I'll use the Jungle Magic*, I decided. *I'll use the magic to get us out of this jam.*

I raised the head slowly in front of me. I opened my mouth to call out the secret word.

But I was stopped when I caught Aunt Benna's glance.

She was signaling me with her eyes. Telling me not to do it.

"What's going on?" Dr. Hawlings demanded, angrily turning to me. "What are you doing?"

"Don't give it away, Mark," Aunt Benna pleaded. "Don't let them know the secret word."

I lowered the shrunken head. "I won't," I whispered.

"It's okay, Daddy," Kareen said, her eyes on me. "I know the word. Mark told it to me. I can tell you what it is. It's —"

I clamped my hand over Kareen's mouth. "Run!" I cried to Aunt Benna. "Run — now!"

With an angry cry of attack, Aunt Benna lowered her shoulder and barreled into Dr. Hawlings. She roared into him like a football player — and sent him sprawling against the little shack.

He uttered a startled yelp. The flashlight flew out of his hand and rolled across the ground.

I spun away from Kareen and followed my aunt. Our shoes thudded through the tall grass as we ran for the trees.

We were nearly to the edge of the clearing when Carolyn stepped in front of us. "What's your hurry?" she demanded, moving to block our way. "The party is just starting."

Aunt Benna and I whirled around. Dr. Hawlings had moved up behind us. We were trapped.

Carolyn raised her flashlight. Her silvery eyes narrowed at Aunt Benna. Carolyn smiled. A cold, unpleasant smile. "How are you, Benna? We missed you."

"Enough chitchat," Dr. Hawlings muttered, gesturing with his flashlight. "It's too dark to go back to the headquarters. We'll have to spend the night here."

"How cozy," Carolyn said, still smiling that cold smile at Aunt Benna.

Aunt Benna scowled and looked away. "Carolyn, I thought you were my friend."

"We're all good friends here," Dr. Hawlings said. "And good friends like to share. That's why you're going to share the secret of Jungle Magic with us, Benna."

"Never!" my aunt declared, crossing her arms in front of her.

"*Never* isn't a word for friends," Dr. Hawlings scolded. "In the morning, we will go back to the headquarters. Then you will share everything, Benna. You will share all of your secrets. And you will give the Jungle Magic to Carolyn and me."

"Like a good friend," Carolyn added.

"Let's go," Dr. Hawlings said. He put a heavy hand on my back and shoved me toward the little shack. Kareen was sitting on the ground, her collar pulled up, her back leaning against one wall.

"You and Benna — in the shack," Dr. Hawlings ordered, giving me another rough shove. "That way, we can keep an eye on you."

"You're wasting your time, Richard," Aunt Benna told him. She was trying to sound tough, but her voice trembled as she said it.

Dr. Hawlings forced us into the dark shack. Aunt Benna and I stretched out on the floor. Through the cracks in the wall, I could see the darting light of their flashlights.

"Are they going to guard us all night?" I whispered.

Aunt Benna nodded. "We're their prisoners now," she whispered back. She sighed. "But we can't let them have the Jungle Magic. We can't!"

I slid closer to my aunt. "If we don't give it to them," I said softly, "what will they do to us?"

Aunt Benna didn't reply.

"What will they do to us?" I repeated.

She stared down at the floor and didn't answer.

A red ball of a sun was rising in the early morning sky when Dr. Hawlings poked his head into the shack and woke us up.

I had slept only a few minutes. The shack had no floor, and the ground was hard.

Whenever I closed my eyes, I dreamed about the shrunken head in my pocket. I dreamed that I held it in my hand. It blinked its eyes and its lips began to move.

"You are doomed!" it exclaimed in a horrifying, hoarse whisper. *"You are doomed. Doomed. Doomed!"*

Aunt Benna and I scrambled out of the shack, stretching and yawning. Even though the sun was still low over the trees, the air already felt hot and wet.

My whole body ached from lying on the hard ground. My shirt was damp and smelly. My stomach growled. I scratched my neck and discovered it was covered with mosquito bites.

Not one of the great mornings.

And it wasn't going to get any better.

We walked for hours through the sweltering jungle. Carolyn and Kareen led the way. Dr. Hawlings walked behind Aunt Benna and me, making sure we didn't try to escape.

No one said a word. The only sounds were the cries of animals, the chirping of birds overhead, and the swish of the tall weeds and grass as we pushed through.

Swarms of white gnats flew up off the path, swirling together like small tornadoes. The sun beamed down through the trees, burning the back of my neck.

When we finally made it back to the row of cabins, I was hot, sweaty, starving, and dying of thirst.

Dr. Hawlings shoved Aunt Benna and me into an empty cabin. He slammed the door behind us and locked it.

The cabin had two folding chairs and a small bed without sheets or blankets. I dropped down wearily onto the bare mattress. "What is he going to do to us?"

Aunt Benna bit her lip. "Don't worry," she said softly. "I'll figure something out." She crossed the small room and tried the window. It was either stuck or bolted from the outside.

"Maybe we can break the glass," I suggested.

"No, he'll hear it," Aunt Benna replied.

I rubbed the back of my neck. The mosquito bites were itching like crazy. I wiped sweat off my forehead with the back of my hand.

The door opened. Kareen entered, carrying two small bottles of water. She tossed one to me and one to my aunt. Then she turned quickly, closed the door hard behind her, and carefully locked it.

I tilted the bottle to my mouth and gulped down the water without taking a breath. There were a few drops left at the bottom. I sprinkled them over the top of my head. Then I tossed the bottle to the floor.

"What are we going to do?" I asked Aunt Benna.

She was sitting in one of the folding chairs, her feet resting on the other. She raised a finger to her lips. "*Ssshhh.*"

Outside, I heard the rattle of machinery. A metallic clang. I heard the rush of water from a hose.

I hurried to the window and peered out. But it faced the wrong way. I couldn't see anything.

"We've had one lucky break," Aunt Benna murmured.

I stared at her. "Excuse me?"

"One lucky break," she repeated. "Hawlings didn't take away the shrunken head. It was so dark last night, I don't think he saw it."

I pulled the head out from my pocket. The black hair had become tangled. I started to smooth it back.

"Put it away, Mark," Aunt Benna ordered sharply. "We don't want Hawlings to see it. He doesn't know that you need the head for Jungle Magic."

"This particular head?" I asked, shoving it back in the pocket. "Only this head?"

Aunt Benna nodded. "Yes. That head and the magic word. The word I gave you when I hypnotized you. When you were four."

The head's black hair fell over my pocket. I carefully tucked it inside.

Outside, I heard another metallic clank. I heard a splash. The roar of water grew louder.

"We are in terrible danger," Aunt Benna said softly. "You will have to use the Jungle Magic to save us, Mark."

I felt a chill of fear. But I muttered, "No problem."

"Wait till I give you the signal," Aunt Benna instructed. "When I blink my eyes three times, pull the shrunken head out and shout the word. Keep watching me. Watch for the signal — okay?"

Before I could reply, the door burst open. Dr. Hawlings and Carolyn hurried in, their faces grim.

Dr. Hawlings carried a large silvery pistol. "Outside," he ordered, waving the pistol at Aunt Benna and me.

Carolyn led the way down the row of cabins. She turned and made us stop behind the main headquarters building. Kareen stood against the wall, a wide-brimmed straw hat pulled down over her eyes.

The sun beamed down. The back of my neck prickled and itched.

Huddling close to my aunt, I squinted into the bright sunlight. To my right, the big pile of shrunken heads came into focus.

The dark eyes on the leathery, green-and-brown heads seemed to stare at me. The mouths were all twisted in ugly expressions of anger and horror.

I turned away from the terrifying pile of tiny heads — to see something even more terrifying.

An enormous black pot stood behind the headquarters building. Water brimmed over the top, bubbling and boiling.

The pot stood on some kind of electric burner. Like a stove burner. It glared red hot. The boiling water inside the pot bubbled and steamed.

I turned to Aunt Benna and caught the fear on her face. "You can't do this!" she screamed to Dr. Hawlings. "You know you can't get away with this!"

"I don't want to hurt you," Dr. Hawlings said calmly, without any emotion at all. A smile spread over his face. "I don't want to harm you, Benna. I just want to own the Jungle Magic."

I kept my eyes locked on my aunt. Waiting for her signal. Waiting for the three blinks that meant I should go into action.

110

"Give me the Jungle Magic," Dr. Hawlings insisted.

Carolyn stepped up beside him, hands on her waist. "Give it to us, Benna. We don't want trouble. We really don't."

"No!" The word shot out of my aunt's mouth. "No! No! No! You both know that I will never give up the secret of Jungle Magic. Not to you. Not ever!"

Carolyn sighed. "Please, Benna. Don't make it difficult."

My aunt stared back at her. "Never," she murmured.

Aunt Benna blinked.

I swallowed hard, watching for two more blinks.

No. Not the signal. Not yet.

Dr. Hawlings stepped forward. "Please, Benna. I'm giving you one last chance. Tell us the secret — now."

Aunt Benna shook her head.

"Then I have no choice," Dr. Hawlings said, shaking his head. "Since you two are the only ones in the world who know the secret, you are both too dangerous. The secret must die with you."

"Wh-what are you going to do to us?" I blurted out.

"We're going to shrink your heads," Dr. Hawlings replied.

28

The pot hissed as water boiled over the side. I stared in horror at the billows of steam rising up over the pot.

Was he really going to shrink our heads?

Was I going to end up shriveled and leathery, with a head the size of a doorknob?

I forced my legs to stop wobbling and stared at Aunt Benna. Stared at her. Stared hard. Watching her eyes. Waiting for the three blinks.

Hurry! I pleaded silently. *Hurry — before he tosses us into the boiling water!*

Kareen watched in silence. What was she thinking? I wondered. I couldn't see her expression. Her face was hidden under the brim of the straw hat.

"Benna, one last chance," Dr. Hawlings said softly. "Because I like you. And I like your nephew. Don't let me harm your nephew, Benna. Do it for him, okay? Tell me the secret — for Mark's sake."

"It isn't worth it, Benna," Carolyn chimed in. "It will be so easy for you to give the Jungle Magic to us."

"I — I can't," Aunt Benna stammered.

"Then we have no choice," Dr. Hawlings said, almost sadly. "The boy goes in first."

He took a step toward me.

Aunt Benna blinked. Once. Twice. Three times.

Finally!

With a trembling hand, I tugged the head from my pocket.

I raised it in front of me. I opened my mouth to shout the secret word.

But Dr. Hawlings swiped the head from my hand.

He grabbed it away — and tossed it onto the big pile of heads.

Then he dove for me, reaching out to grab me with both hands.

I ducked out from under him.

And threw myself onto the disgusting pile of heads.

I began frantically sorting through them with both hands. Picking one up, tossing it aside. Grabbing the next one. The next one. The next one.

They felt sticky and warm. Hard as baseballs. The hair brushed my hands. The dark eyes stared up at me blankly. They were so ugly, my stomach tightened. My breath came in wheezing gasps.

113

Behind me, I could hear my aunt struggling with Dr. Hawlings. Wrestling with him. Trying to keep him away from me.

I heard Carolyn's shouts. Kareen's cries of alarm.

I had to find *my* shrunken head.

I had to find it before Dr. Hawlings broke free of my aunt and grabbed me.

I picked one up. Tossed it down. Picked up another. Tossed it down.

How could I find mine?

Which one was it?

Which one? Which one?

I grabbed a head. Saw ants crawling over its cheeks.

Picked up another.

It stared at me with glassy black eyes.

Picked up another.

It had a long white scratch on its ear.

I started to toss it back onto the pile.

But stopped.

A white scratch on its ear?

Yes! Mine had a scratch! My sister, Jessica — she scratched it back home!

Yes! This head was mine!

"Thank you, Jessica!" I cried at the top of my lungs.

With an angry cry, Dr. Hawlings dove at me. He wrapped his arms around me and started to drag me off the pile of heads.

"Kah-lee-ah!" I shouted, holding on tightly to the shrunken head. *My* shrunken head. "Kah-lee-ah!"

Will it save Aunt Benna and me? I wondered. *Will the Jungle Magic work this time?*

Dr. Hawlings still had his arms around my shoulders. He was still trying to pull me toward the boiling pot.

"Kah-lee-ah!" I screamed.

His hands slid away.

They seemed to shrink. His arms seemed to shrink into his body.

"Huh?" I uttered a startled cry when I realized that *he* was shrinking. Dr. Hawlings's entire body was shrinking, growing smaller and smaller!

I raised my eyes to Kareen and Carolyn. They were shrinking, too. Shrinking down to the ground.

Kareen disappeared under the straw hat. Then she came running out from under the brim. A tiny Kareen, about the size of a mouse.

All three of them — Kareen, Carolyn, and Dr. Hawlings — scampered over the grass. Mouse-sized. Squeaking angrily in tiny mouse voices.

I stood beside the pile of heads and watched them scurry over the ground. Squeaking and squealing. I watched them until they disappeared into the jungle.

Then I turned back to Aunt Benna. "It worked!" I cried. "The Jungle Magic — it saved us!"

She rushed forward and wrapped me in a hug. "You did it, Mark. You did it! The jungle is safe now! The whole world is safe!"

There were more hugs when Aunt Benna flew me home. Hugs from Mom — and even Jessica.

They met us at the airport. Then Mom drove us home for a big welcome-home dinner. I had so many stories to tell, I started telling them in the car. And I didn't stop talking until way past dinner.

It was nearly bedtime when Aunt Benna led me into the den. She closed the door behind us. Then she sat me down on the couch.

She sat down beside me. "Look into my eyes," she said softly. "Look deeply, Mark. Very deeply."

I raised my eyes to hers. "What are you going to do?" I asked.

I didn't hear her reply.

As I stared into her eyes, the room grew fuzzy. The colors all seemed to shift and blur. I thought I saw the posters on the den wall flipping over and over. I thought I saw the chairs and coffee table sliding across the floor.

After a while, the room came back into focus. Aunt Benna smiled at me. "There," she said, squeezing my hand. "You're back to normal, Mark."

"Huh?" I squinted at her. "What do you mean?"

"No more Jungle Magic," she explained. "I took it back. You're a normal boy again."

"You mean, if I shout 'Kah-lee-ah' nothing will happen?" I asked.

"That's right." She smiled at me, still holding my hand. "I took back the magic. The shrunken head has no powers. And you have no powers. You never have to worry about it again."

She stood up, yawning. "It's getting late. Bedtime, don't you think?"

I nodded. "Yeah. I guess." I was still thinking about how I didn't have Jungle Magic anymore. "Aunt Benna?"

"Yes?"

"Can I keep the shrunken head?"

"Of course," she replied, tugging me to my feet. "Keep the shrunken head. As a souvenir. That way, you will always remember your jungle adventure."

"I don't think I could forget it too easily," I replied. Then I said good night and made my way to bed.

The next morning, I woke up early and pulled on my clothes as fast as I could. I couldn't wait to get to school and show off the shrunken head to Eric and Joel and all the other kids.

I gulped down my cornflakes and chugged my orange juice. I strapped on my backpack. Called good-bye to Mom. Grabbed the shrunken head and headed out the door.

Holding the head carefully in my hand, I started to jog along the sidewalk. It was a bright, sunny day. The air smelled warm and sweet.

My school is only three blocks from my house. But as I jogged along, it seemed like miles.

I couldn't wait to get there and show off to everyone.

I couldn't wait to tell my friends about all my jungle adventures.

I could see the school in the next block. And I could see a bunch of kids hanging out by the front door.

As I ran across the street, I suddenly felt the head move in my hand.

It twitched.

"Huh?" I let out a gasp and stared down at it.

The eyes blinked, then stared up at me. The lips closed, then opened again. "Hey, kid," the head growled. "Let *me* tell the part about the tiger!"

BEHIND THE SCREAMS

HOW I GOT MY SHRUNKEN HEAD

CONTENTS

Bonus material written and compiled
by Matthew D. Payne

About the Author

R.L. Stine's books are read all over the world. So far, his books have sold more than 300 million copies, making him one of the most popular children's authors in history. Besides Goosebumps, R.L. Stine has written the teen series Fear Street, the funny series Rotten School, as well as the Mostly Ghostly series, The Nightmare Room series, and the two-book thriller *Dangerous Girls*. R.L. Stine lives in New York with his wife, Jane, and Minnie, his King Charles spaniel. You can learn more about him at www.RLStine.com.

Q & A with R.L. Stine

How long could you survive in the jungle, alone and without supplies?

R.L. Stine (RLS): *Not long. I don't like leaving my crypt—I mean, apartment.*

Do you own a shrunken head?

RLS: *I do have a shrunken head . . . my own! You don't think you could dream up all these weird ideas with a normal head, do you?*

Your readers are *dying* to know: What happened to Kareen, Carolyn, and Dr. Hawlings after they were shrunk and ran off into the jungle?

RLS: *I'm dying to know, too. Let me know if any of you ever run into them!*

Your books have given millions of kids goose bumps, but what about you? Have you ever found yourself frightened by your own writing?

RLS: *No, my writing never frightens me. But occasionally I laugh at my own jokes. Sometimes I crack myself up!*

What else are you frightened of? Large spiders? Dark basements? Flying?

RLS: *Just about anything can be scary. And often things that are very ordinary are the scariest things of all. Like dolls. Children play with dolls. They're sweet, right? But many books and movies have made dolls seem really creepy. Frankly, I don't trust dolls. Do you?*

If you were a superhero, what would your superpower be?

RLS: *I'd be Steel-Finger, because I have typed all of my books with just one finger. You should see it! It's all bent and funny looking from typing three hundred books!*

Things are getting crazy in HorrorLand! In Goosebumps HorrorLand #10: *Help! We Have Strange Powers!* we go even deeper into this mysterious theme park. What sort of special powers do the kids have, and why do they need help?

RLS: *They need all the help they can get—especially when they come up against two new supervillains who are definitely not kid friendly.*

To find out what R.L. Stine thinks about ventriloquist's dummies, pick up the special collector's edition of Goosebumps: *NIGHT OF THE LIVING DUMMY*.

Recipe for Shrunken Heads

Creating real shrunken heads is tough work! You have to remove the skull ever so carefully, boil the skin just perfectly, and spend hours and hours rolling hot stones and sand around in the ever-shrinking head. Who has time for that?

Want an easier way to create a shrunken head? Then follow the recipe below.

WARNING: *Please ask an adult for help!*
This recipe involves carving tools.

Ingredients & Tools:

½ cup lemon juice

½ tablespoon salt

small bowl

spoon

one large apple

vegetable peeler

butter knife

toothpick

small plate

STEP 1 Mix ½ cup lemon juice with ½ tablespoon salt in the small bowl. Set aside.

STEP 2 Peel the apple with the vegetable peeler. Using the spoon, coat the apple with some of the lemon juice and salt mixture: It will keep your apple from browning while you work on it.

STEP 3 Using the butter knife, carve a face into the apple: eyes, nose, mouth, and ears. Don't worry about details—think big: deep eyes, big nose, and a big grimace. As the apple shrinks, so will your carving. You can use the toothpick for any small details you would like to add. If you're feeling extra creative, place cloves into the eye sockets, add pieces of pasta or rice for teeth, and anything else you can think of!

STEP 4 Coat your apple with the lemon juice and salt mixture one more time: This will keep your shrunken head from rotting. Who wants a rotten head? Nobody!

STEP 5 Put your apple on a small plate or drying rack in a warm and dry spot in your house. It will slowly shrink and shrink and shrink, until a week or two later . . .

You have your own shrunken head!

Feel free to decorate your head with yarn for hair, or use markers to add eyebrows and other features. Can you think of any other ways to decorate your shrunken head?

Be creative and have fun!

Quicksand Survival Guide

Have you ever had that sinking feeling? You know the one—you're walking along in the jungle and suddenly you find that you can't go on . . . because the ground has started swallowing you!

Well, fear not!

Although books, movies, and television make quicksand look like a death trap, it's actually quite easy to survive a quicksand attack. All it takes is time and patience.

RULE #1 Don't step into quicksand in the first place! Quicksand can be found just about anywhere that's moist: near lake shores, by rivers and streams, at the beach, in marshes, and in mudflats during low tide. When you're out in these areas, carry a walking stick, so if you have any doubts about the firmness of the ground in front of you, you can poke it!

RULE #2 If you find yourself stuck in quicksand, don't thrash around. You'll just sink faster if you do. So keep a cool head. Slow and steady wins the race.

RULE #3 Most patches of quicksand are quite shallow. If you've gotten the bottom half of your body stuck, make circular motions with your legs to create space in the quicksand and free yourself.

RULE #4 If the sand is deep, lay back, relax, and enjoy your day at the quicksand beach. No, really.

It's impossible to pull yourself out while standing straight—lay back as if you were floating on the surface of water and you might be able to slowly move your way to a dry piece of land. And remember to relax and do everything *slowly*—otherwise you'll find yourself too tired to go on.

RULE #5 Once you've laid back on the surface of the quicksand, spread your arms and legs to help you float, just like you would in water.

RULE #6 Breathe deeply. Just like in water, if you fill up your lungs with air, you'll float better. So take long, deep breaths.

Eventually, you'll find your way to a dry patch and you can slowly wiggle your way out!

Now, please, do yourself a favor and just remember RULE #1!

Jungle Creatures of the Night

As Mark knows all too well, night in the jungle belongs to the creatures. And, boy, does it get loud! But what is making all that noise?

FROGS compete to be heard in the wet jungle at night—it's not surprising to find hundreds of frogs in a section of jungle the size of a big backyard, and all of them have a distinct croak. Luckily for Mark, most frogs aren't dangerous. Some are poisonous, but none of them have a habit of jumping into human mouths.

The male **HAMMER-HEADED BAT** of the Congo is built for loud **HONKING**. Where most bats let out barely perceptible squeaking, this one can cut through the noise of the jungle! These bats eat fruit and are harmless to humans (unless your head tastes like a mango).

Many other insects and animals add to the symphony of the night, but it's the *quiet* creatures that you should be fearful of. They're the ones that can really creep up on you.

Although most people think **VAMPIRE BATS** come from Transylvania, they actually call the jungle their home. They quietly creep up on animals in the night and drink their blood, usually while the animal is asleep. Their teeth are so sharp and small that their bite doesn't wake the sleeping animal! Vampire bats consume half their weight in blood in about twenty minutes and then take off to roost and digest their meal.

And that's not the only blood-sucking creature in the jungle; there are **VAMPIRE MOTHS** (no, we're not kidding) and kissing bugs. The **KISSING BUG** gets its name from its nasty habit of biting tender parts of a human's face, like the lips, to draw and drink blood.

Some of the stealthiest killers live in the jungle: big cats like **JAGUARS**, **LEOPARDS**, and **TIGERS**. Jaguars are especially fond of the deepest jungles and will stalk and ambush their prey—silently creeping up and pouncing—rather than chasing it. **FIERCE FACT**: The jaguar has the most powerful bite of *any* big cat (even more powerful than the lion's) and has a unique habit of biting right through the skull of its prey!

WE CAN SEE YOU! Some nocturnal primates, such as the **AYE-AYE** and the **TARSIER,** have huge buggy eyes to see in the dark jungle night. Although completely harmless, they look almost alien. The tarsier is especially creepy looking, with gnarled, witchlike hands!

GLOW IN THE DARK FUNGUS. In some jungles, a **GLOWING FUNGUS** grows on the trunks of trees, giving them a mysterious shine.

Say the Magic Words

Do you know the magic words?

Kah-lee-ah! Chant this word to unleash Jungle Magic!

Karru marri odonna loma molonu! These five words have an eerie and often surprising effect on dummies, like Slappy.

Hocus-pocus, Presto chango, Abracadabra, and **Alakazam** are all common words spoken by magicians around the globe while making a magic trick happen.

Voilà! (Pronounced VWAA-LAA!) Another word used by magicians, but usually as they reveal the result of the magic.

Open Sesame. A phrase that opens a magically sealed cave filled with treasure.

And don't forget . . .

Please. This is the magic word that everyone wants to hear. It's perfect for practicing the magic trick known as "being polite."

Interested in other magical forces?
Then check out

#10: HELP! WE HAVE STRANGE POWERS!

The all-new, all-terrifying thrill ride from R.L. Stine.

Jillian and Jackson freak out when they suddenly realize
they can read people's thoughts. But the trick turns to
terror when the twins are stalked by a strange scientist
who wants to know exactly what's on their minds. Will the
twins ever lead normal lives again?

Not in Horrorland they won't. There are free meals, free
games, and free falls down the Doom Slide. Someone's
watching their every step. But are they friend or foe?

NOW A MAJOR
MOTION PICTURE

JACK BLACK

Goosebumps

VILLAGE
ROADSHOW

THIS FILM IS NOT YET RATED
FOR FUTURE INFO GO TO

f /GoosebumpsTheMovie

SCHOLASTIC

COLUMBIA
PICTURES

REVENGE OF THE LIVING DUMMY
R.L. STINE

CREEP FROM THE DEEP
R.L. STINE

MONSTER BLOOD FOR BREAKFAST!
R.L. STINE

THE SCREAM OF THE HAUNTED MASK
R.L. STINE

DR. MANIAC VS. ROBBY SCHWARTZ
R.L. STINE

WHO'S YOUR MUMMY?
R.L. STINE

MY FRIENDS CALL ME MONSTER
R.L. STINE

SAY CHEESE - AND DIE SCREAMING!
R.L. STINE

WELCOME TO CAMP SLITHER
R.L. STINE

■ SCHOLASTIC

SCHOLASTIC and associated logos
are trademarks and/or registered
trademarks of Scholastic Inc.

www.EnterHorrorLand.com

GBHL19B

THE SCARIEST PLACE ON EARTH!

HELP! WE HAVE STRANGE POWERS!
R.L. STINE

ESCAPE FROM HORRORLAND
R.L. STINE

THE STREETS OF PANIC PARK
R.L. STINE

WHEN THE GHOST DOG HOWLS
R.L. STINE

LITTLE SHOP OF HAMSTERS
R.L. STINE

HEADS, YOU LOSE!
R.L. STINE

WEIRDO HALLOWEEN
R.L. STINE

THE WIZARD OF OOZE
R.L. STINE

SLAPPY NEW YEAR!
R.L. STINE

THE HORROR AT CHILLER HOUSE
R.L. STINE

■ SCHOLASTIC

www.EnterHorrorLand.com

SCHOLASTIC and associated logos
are trademarks and/or registered
trademarks of Scholastic Inc.

GBHL19B

The Original Bone-Chilling Series

—with Exclusive
Author Interviews!

Goosebumps NIGHT of the LIVING DUMMY
R.L. STINE

Goosebumps DEEP TROUBLE
R.L. STINE

Goosebumps MONSTER BLOOD
R.L. STINE

Goosebumps The HAUNTED MASK
R.L. STINE

Goosebumps ONE DAY at HORRORLAND
R.L. STINE

Goosebumps The CURSE of the MUMMY'S TOMB
R.L. STINE

Goosebumps BE CAREFUL WHAT YOU WISH FOR
R.L. STINE

Goosebumps SAY CHEESE and DIE!
R.L. STINE

Goosebumps The HORROR at CAMP JELLYJAM
R.L. STINE

Goosebumps HOW I GOT MY SHRUNKEN HEAD
R.L. STINE

SCHOLASTIC

SCHOLASTIC and associated logos
are trademarks and/or registered
trademarks of Scholastic Inc.

www.scholastic.com/goosebumps

GBCL22

R. L. Stine's Fright Fest!
Now with Splat Stats and More!

■SCHOLASTIC Read them all!

SCHOLASTIC and associated logos
are trademarks and/or registered
trademarks of Scholastic Inc.

www.scholastic.com/goosebumps

GBCL22

Catch the MOST WANTED Goosebumps® villains UNDEAD OR ALIVE!

SCHOLASTIC, GOOSEBUMPS and associated logos
are trademarks and/or registered trademarks
of Scholastic Inc. All rights reserved.

SCHOLASTIC
scholastic.com/goosebumps

Available in print
and eBook editions

GBMW9